never too SOON

To all the girls who feel they're not good enough…

You deserve more than you'll ever receive.
Never settle for less than spectacular.

Publisher © Chelle Bliss August 1st 2023
Edited by Lisa A. Hollett
Proofread by Read By Rose & Shelley Carlton
Cover Design © Chelle Bliss
Cover Photo © Eric Battershell
Cover Model: Burton Hughes

To all the girls who feel they're not good enough…

You deserve more than you'll ever receive.
Never settle for less than spectacular.

Publisher © Chelle Bliss August 1st 2023

Edited by Lisa A. Hollett

Proofread by Read By Rose & Shelley Carlton

Cover Design © Chelle Bliss

Cover Photo © Eric Battershell

Cover Model: Burton Hughes

CHAPTER 1
GRACE

I CANNOT START my day without an extra-large cup of coffee. And on days like today, the only coffee that will do is the stuff made by my sister-in-law, Chloe, at the bookstore next to my tattoo shop.

I crash through the door of the bookstore, expecting to see my brother's wife behind the counter, looking nerdy and precious as she always does in her cargo pants and boots. Instead, I'm smacked with a sight I wish I could unsee.

Tucked into the back pockets of Chloe's tan cargo pants are my brother's hands, and his face is nuzzled into the crook of her neck.

"Shit, Franco." I halfway cover my eyes, keeping a space between two fingers to see, and stalk to the counter. "It's too early for that."

My brother lifts his face from Chloe's neck, his eyes looking love-drunk and his lips looking disgustingly puffy.

I groan again and wave a hand in front of me. "Don't you both have jobs to do instead of groping each other?"

Franco snorts and smooths back his hair. The bastard has the nerve to look smug when I'm the one whose eyeballs are forever sullied.

"Did you see the sign on the door?" He jerks a thumb toward the entrance that I just burst through. "Store emergency. The plumbing is all jacked up. Carpet's wet. The whole nine. Chloe had to close for the day while she waits for a plumber."

Chloe looks at me with a sweet grin. "We're closed to the public, Gracie, but I figured you'd come in for your coffee. That's why I left the door unlocked. You're right on time. I have it ready and waiting."

"I'm going to come behind that counter and smooch your face off. I love you so much right now," I say on a sigh.

Instead, I blow Chloe a kiss and watch as she adjusts her clothes while she runs back into the small kitchen to pour my coffee.

I slap my brother on the shoulder, then rest my elbows on the front counter. "You two are gross. Isn't that shit supposed to end after you get married?"

Franco ruffles my hair. "Jealous much?"

I smack him a second time. He's a jerk.

"So, what the hell happened to the plumbing?"

Franco frowns. "Don't know. Chloe doesn't think it happened here, though. I took a peek when I shut off the water. Might be a building-wide problem. Tree roots breaking the sewer line or maybe one of the other tenants clogged the drains. You guys okay next door?"

I shake my head. "I haven't opened the shop yet. I came here first." This news makes a sucky morning even suckier. "Fuck," I sigh and rake a hand through my hair.

Franco lifts a brow at me. "You're extra salty today. You okay?"

But my eldest brother's right. On top of my normal snark, today, I've got anxiety practically oozing from my pores.

What's going on with me is something I haven't shared with anyone yet. I'm definitely not ready for that at this hour.

Franco has always been the most helicopter brother of the three male Bianchis, but this… If any one of them found out what was going on with me, I'd never hear the end of it.

"Earth to Gracie." Franco cocks his head, studying my face as though he can read my mind.

Thank God that's not a thing. I'd never have a moment's peace if my mother or brothers could see inside my head.

"Just need my coffee," I say dismissively. "I didn't sleep well last night."

"Me either. I was up half the night with Violet." Franco leans across the counter and taps my nose with a finger. "You want to come to our place for dinner tonight? You got plans?"

I shrug. "I'm working until seven. We'll see how I

feel. If I can't keep my eyes open, it's better if I go home after work than come over. Or else I might end up sleeping on your couch."

Franco stares at me with a puzzled look on his face, but then Chloe comes back with an extra-large cup of coffee in each hand.

"You looked like you could use a double today," she says sweetly.

I take the cups, lean close, and smooch her on the cheek. "You're the best, sis."

Her face lights up when I call her that. She's loved it since I did it the first time.

I'm juggling the two paper cups when it hits me that someone is missing from the bookstore. "Where's the dog?" I call over my shoulder.

Franco gives Chloe a kiss on the cheek in an annoyingly long goodbye and then walks around the counter. "In my truck," he says. "That's why I'm here. When Chloe got here and discovered the mess, we figured it'd be safer to keep the dog away from the plumber and whatnot. I'm taking her back with me to the shop."

The lightbulb goes on in my brain, despite my lack of caffeine. Now his being at the bookstore in the middle of the day makes perfect sense.

He yanks open the door for me so I don't spill my coffees.

"Give her ear scratches for me," I call after Franco before glancing over my shoulder again. "Thanks, Chloe."

I only have to walk about ten paces to get to the

place I work. The Body Shop is the only tattoo shop in Star Falls. It just so happens to have the same name as the only strip club in the county, which has been the source of a lot of jokes over the years. Especially during the short time my brother Vito was married to a dancer with the stage name "Exotic," aka Michelle.

My parents were far from thrilled when I decided to apprentice at a tattoo shop, but I know better than to judge people by what they do for a living, what they drive… All that crap doesn't mean jack shit. Sometimes the choices we make are…the best we can do. Being an adult is damn tough.

I have good parents. I come from an amazing family. But we never had a lot. My brother Vito and I both still live at home, and it's not just because my dad's cooking is to freaking die for. I could go home whenever I wanted a meal. Big Sunday dinners are a requirement for all the Bianchi kids. And now Chloe, too.

I lived alone for a short time and learned a lot of lessons very quickly. I don't like to think too much about that time, but there are days—like today—when all I can think about is what's coming up next. The next doctor's appointment. The next test. The next call to my insurance company about co-pays and approvals.

That's why I didn't give a shit if my brother married a stripper. Michelle was cool, and I think she actually loved my brother. Most people have something about them that you can like if you just give them a chance. Bookseller, stripper… Who cares.

Underneath it all, our hearts are what matter.

I have walked literally two steps from the bookshop, lost deep in my thoughts, when I see a man peering through the still-dark windows of The Body Shop.

"Hey, there. Excuse me. Hi?" I call out as I approach the guy. I look him over, trying to assess why he's looking in the window of a store that's obviously closed.

"Oh, hey. Hello." When he turns around, my stomach does that little flippy thing it does every time I see someone with muscles and a wide, sincere smile.

Ughhhhh.

The man is big and, like, rugby-player muscular. Totally yummy.

I know. I've dated athletes. And with all the bodies my hands have worked on over the years, I can tell gym muscles from muscles that can do miraculous things.

I can see this man has a body that is put through a vigorous regimen.

His thighs are crazy muscled. He's wearing shorts but not suburban dad shorts. These are the shorts of a guy who just rolled off a field someplace after scoring a last-second, game-winning goal. One knee has the etched-looking, well-healed scars from some kind of orthopedic repair. And his arms… He's wearing nothing sexy, just a plain soft blue tee, but the thing must be made of the world's finest cotton. It's stretched over defined pecs that would normally make my mouth water.

But God, those arms…*drool.*

I have to stop myself before I turn into an idiotic

puddle of goo. This guy is not *just* my type; he's every stupid stereotype I've ever fallen for in the past.

And, oh, how I've been burned.

As I take him in, he's looking back at me like he's not sure whose turn it is to talk, but if it's his, he might owe me an apology even if he doesn't know why.

"Do you…work here?" he asks, looking from my cups to the shop.

"Sure do," I say. "Here." I thrust both cups of coffee toward him and fumble in my giant silver studded purse for my keys. "You look smart enough to handle this, but just be careful. These are hot," I remind him.

I normally juggle two cups just fine, but if he's a weirdo or a criminal, keeping his hands busy while I open the store feels a lot safer than me having my hands full.

Although the day is clear and sunny, and one scream would no doubt bring Chloe and half of downtown Star Falls running, I refuse to consider that maybe, just maybe, I'm not opposed to the hunky athlete carrying my coffee.

He takes both cups, his lips slightly parted and a confused look on his face.

Wicked cute, this one.

A tangle of brown curls held back from a slightly tanned forehead with a touch of gel. A nice tight shave up the back of his neck. But I stop giving him the once-over and unlock The Body Shop.

Once I return the jangle of keys on my glittery lanyard back to the bottomless pit of my purse, I twist the tablet on the front counter, punch in the security code, and turn up the lights.

"Wow," the guy says, following me in. He scans the cool-gray wallpaper with subtle gold-foil roses, the mid-century-style oak furniture, and the pops of green from a few thriving potted plants. "This is not what I expected of a tattoo shop."

My words come out along with a ferocious glare before I can stop them. "What did you expect? Sweat-stained couches and cracked poster frames with sheets of generic flash? We don't cater to frat boys here." Before he can answer, I give him a look and hold up a finger. "I need to check something. You can set those on the counter."

I walk through a bifold door, planning to secure my purse at my station, when I feel a slosh of water under my boot.

"Fuck. No," I groan. Ahead of me, the floor surrounding the six tattoo stations is flooded. Water at least an inch deep in spots pools around the bays. The floor back here is easy-to-clean strip flooring in a natural honey shade that complements the classic and calming decor. And it's freaking soaked.

My curses echo through the store, and in a heart-beat, I hear the guy from up front push open the bifold door.

"Are you okay?" he asks.

I throw him a dirty look. He's still holding the cups of coffee, but now his sneakers are soaking up who knows what this is.

He looks down at his feet, then back at me, then looks at the cups in his hands.

"Get back," I tell him, careful not to slip as I step through the water. I wave at him to go back up front.

Thankfully, the lobby floor is still dry.

My customer's expensive-looking sneakers squeak as he sets the coffees on the counter. "Do you know where the water shutoff is? I might be able to help."

But I'm too busy digging in my purse for my cell phone to think straight. "I'm calling the building owner," I tell him, panic edging my voice.

"Can I look?" he asks, nodding toward the back room.

I shrug as I pull up the contact for the management company.

The second the voice mail picks up, I start hollering about water flooding the store. I drop as many colorful adjectives and curse words as I possibly can before hanging up.

I dig through my purse for the keys and lock the front door so no one else can walk in on this mess.

When I head into the back room, Mr. Rugby is on his hands and knees. He has taken a pair of black nitrile gloves from someone's station. He's wearing them on his hands as he blots up the water from the floor with a stack of our black shop towels.

"Oh my God," I gasp. "What are you doing?"

He's looking calm, cool, and very confident for a guy who's probably soaked to his ankles in sewage.

He gives me the thumbs-up with a very wet black

glove and does this half-push-up, half-lunge-like move to get from his knees to his feet.

"Shit," he grumbles, and I hear his knee audibly pop as he stands. "Should've taken that a little slower."

"You shouldn't have done any of this," I wave my hand at his cleanup efforts, "at all. You could get sick from crawling around in dirty water."

I'm starting to straight-up panic. Our equipment is sterile. Our workplace meticulously cleaned. We book tattoos by appointment only, and we have more than sufficient time to keep The Body Shop to the highest standards.

Now, the whole place has had a shit wash and has to be sanitized.

I crumple down into the chair at my station, the bottom of my boots submerged in the water. "Holy fuck," I gasp. The reality of the situation is fully hitting me now.

"The news isn't that bad," my knight in shining nitrile gloves says.

He bounces on his squeaky shoes, all smiles and reassurances. He's got the energy of a golden retriever and the deep brown eyes of a heartthrob.

"I think you have an issue with your water inlet valve," he says. "Come look."

I arch a brow at him and shake my head. "What in the fuck is that?"

"Come on," he urges. "I promise. This isn't sewage water or anything like that. If it were, you'd definitely smell it. I'm pretty sure you have an issue with the washing machine. I'll show you."

I throw him a look because if he's planning to murder me or pull anything dodgy, I want him to know I'm not going down without a fight. But I take my life in my hands because we do, after all, have security cameras and follow him to the back of the store. We have two bathrooms—one we reserve for customers and one marked *Employees Only.*

The employee bathroom is huge. At the back is a washer and dryer where we clean and dry the shop towels right here on the premises.

"I shut off the water to the toilets and sinks in both bathrooms, but I'm pretty sure that valve back here is the problem." He's pointing at the colored handles and twisty knobs with hoses installed in the wall behind the washing machine and dryer. I'm sure he thinks I understand, but my mind is a mess.

The shop is flooded.

We have a schedule full of appointments today. Clients who might already be waiting at the front door.

It might be our fault that the bookshop flooded.

Shit.

Or it might be some other tenant's fault, which means there will be arguments with the property owner, cleanup, and a whole lot of headaches we don't need.

And worst of all, I haven't even had my coffee yet.

"So, you'll definitely need a plumber," he finishes, as I realize I haven't been listening to any of what he explained. "But I think this is just tap water. Not sewage. A couple of towels and a mop, you'll be back in business."

I know there is no way this could be that easy, but somehow his cheerfulness makes it hard to keep frowning. "You drink coffee?" I ask.

He looks at me curiously.

"Cream and sugar?"

When he gives the cutest little nod, looking so adorably trusting, I head to the front of the shop, grab one of my extra-larges, and walk back to where he's standing. I offer one to my hero and drop down in my chair. "Have a seat," I say. "And drink up. You deserve it."

CHAPTER 2
RYDER

THE SPITFIRE FLAILING her arms while she tells the owner of the building about the flooding has me biting back a grin.

But I shouldn't even be here. I don't know what drove me to stop in front of a tattoo shop, of all places, today.

Well, that's not true. I know why I came here, and I know why I came *today*.

But I never once imagined that I'd actually go inside. Being dragged in and force-fed coffee by a woman with raven-black hair is the last thing I imagined when I decided to get a tattoo.

"No," the woman snaps into the phone. She's finished a full cup of coffee and seems to be calming. "Echo wasn't on the schedule until three today, when I am scheduled for my first client. I'm here alone right now." She looks at me as she says that but then raises a dramatic brow. "Not alone-alone," she corrects. "The customer who shut off the water is here."

She paces the lobby until she finishes her conversation.

"All right. All right. I know, I know. I will. Bye." Finally, she hangs up the phone and jams the device into the rear pocket of shredded black jeans, then she turns those startling gray eyes on me.

"So," she says, "I've got to close the shop. This is going to take some time to clean and investigate. I need to call my appointments and get things canceled. It's going to be a clusterfuck in here."

I understand without her saying it. She's asking me to leave. I take another sip of the coffee and nod. "Understood," I say. I start walking to the door, but the squeak of my drenched shoes is so loud, I begin to laugh.

"Your shoes." She scurries around the counter and grabs my arm.

I look down at her, at the softness of her skin on mine. Heat pools in my gut as she quickly pulls her hand away.

"I…uh. I should replace your shoes," she says, her words tumbling out in a rush. "I'm so sorry. They got ruined just because you were trying to do a good thing."

I shake my head. "Nah. Not a problem. Both these shoes and I have been through much worse. They'll dry." I lift the cup in mock salute. "Consider us even. Really good coffee. Best I've had in Star Falls yet."

She smiles, and the action softens her considerably.

She's got jet-black hair that doesn't look dyed. It's glossy and cut in long layers that frame her face. She's wearing a loose-fitting tank top with a skull made out of roses on it and a tighter tank underneath. It's hard not to notice the cleavage that seems to want to be anywhere but hidden. Her arms and the backs of her hands are covered in tattoos. She looks and sounds scary as hell, but up close, when she smiles, she's pure sugar.

"My brother's wife," she explains, hooking a thumb over her shoulder. "Next door. They make the best coffee in town. And peanut butter crisps. But you got to get there early because they sell out fast."

I nod in thanks. "I'm an early riser," I tell her, not sure why I'm offering so much personal information to a total stranger. "I'll have to try them someday."

I give her a smile, but something stops me from grabbing the door handle. I should go. I mean, I *should* just leave. What I came here for is something I definitely don't need. Hell, I'm not even sure I want a tattoo. But I'm here now and have a few more hours to myself. I can afford to linger. Even if it is just to talk to a beautiful woman for a couple more minutes.

It's been so long…

And with this woman, it feels easy. Way too easy.

The way she's looking at me feels like she's thinking about saying more too. With just a lift of one of those perfectly shaped brows, she's expressive and thoughtful. I'd always know where I stood with a woman like this, and that feeling intrigues me.

"Did you have an appointment?" she asks, sounding both a little confused and a little suspicious.

"No," I admit. "No appointment."

"But you came here for a tattoo?" she presses.

Her gaze skating over my body is as sensuous as a caress. My skin heats under her appraisal.

"Yeah…" I laugh awkwardly. "I did want a tattoo. I still do, maybe? I thought I'd come in, look at a few pictures, get ignored by some hipster at the front desk, and feel ashamed enough of myself to never think about getting a tattoo again."

"Why would you be ashamed?" she asks again with that brow.

I consider her question, and I debate being honest. I'd actually prepared an answer just in case anyone did ask me what I was doing here. It felt better having something prepared so I wouldn't be surprised into giving anyone the whole truth. At least, not before I am ready.

I hold up my arms, the last dregs of the coffee sloshing in the cup I'm still holding. "I'm a virgin," I admit. "Blank canvas. Clean slate. I have no clue what I'm doing."

She softens even more, and if it's possible, she grows even more gorgeous. Her eyes are an inviting gray, like the soothing, welcoming gray of the wallpaper. She has heavy wings of eyeliner that accentuate the shape of her eyes and the stark black peaks of her brows. She's beautiful and unlike anyone I've ever known.

"Does anybody?" she asks. Her words are serious, and somehow the sincerity in them makes my heart rate speed up.

There was a time when I thought I had all the answers. A time when every moment of my life was scheduled and full and happy and safe.

Until it wasn't and nothing made any sense.

I know I'm not the only one who's lost a hell of a lot at far too young an age. But every battle is different. And what I've learned over the last couple of years is that no playbook can prepare you for every possibility. Foul balls, penalties, injuries, and illness...

All of that is the chaos of life.

The cost of being alive.

I'm guessing by her reaction that this woman's bright colors mask a darkness underneath. No, scratch that. It's not darkness. There's wisdom behind those gray eyes. Maybe the same kind of weariness that I recognize in myself.

"You got that right," I say, shaking my head. "One day you think you're going to get your first tattoo, and the next thing you know, the only new colors in your life are the water stains on your sneakers."

Her mouth falls open, and both brows get moving. I hold up a hand before she can insist on replacing my trainers again. "Kidding," I tell her. "Humor. It's a coping mechanism. No harm done."

I take a step closer to the door.

She smiles then. Her teeth are white, her lips full and perfectly painted on with dark red lipstick.

I've never kissed anyone who wore lipstick like that.

Even on our wedding day, Elizabeth went for the natural look. She was always beautiful in my eyes.

My life is no longer that of a happily married man, father, and coach.

I'm a widower.

A struggling single dad.

And I'm about to start a new job in a new town miles from my old support system.

Miles from the memories.

This place is supposed to be my new horizon.

But I'm in a tattoo shop, holding an empty coffee cup, and my feet are soaking wet.

Hardly the bright new start I expected when I moved here. Something I thought Elizabeth would want for me as much as I want it for myself.

The tattoo artist has her eyes narrowed and her chin lifted. Her plush lips are pressed together as if she's trying to figure out what to say next. I spare her the effort.

"Best of luck with your plumbing. And thanks again for the coffee." I reach to open the door, but she's locked the dead bolt from inside.

She has the keys around her neck, the tangle of brass and silver dangling between her breasts as she leans past me, selects the right key, and unlocks the door.

As she steps back, I smell her hair and the sweet

fragrance of coffee as she exhales. I don't know what I expected a tattoo artist to smell like, but the scent that fills my nose is soft and gentle. Like I'm in a luxury spa or a salon. Elizabeth never used fancy products in her hair. Nothing that could drag me in, seduce me, and envelop me in a soft cloud that promised to carry me away from everything real and hard.

"Hi, hey." A very tall, curvy redhead with a distinctive retro-looking haircut comes hustling up the block on open toe wedge heels. She's exactly the sort of woman you'd expect to see at a tattoo shop. "Are you a customer? I'm sorry I was running late."

I nod. "Right place, wrong time. I'm just heading out. I think things are under control in there."

"Thank you," she says. "Did Gracie get your number? Can we reschedule you? If you decide to get a tattoo, I'll work out a discount with whatever artist you choose."

I commit her name to memory. *Gracie.*

I would have loved an excuse to give her my number, but I'm not even sure I want a tattoo. What I would love is the chance to see her again, though.

"You have a lot going on. I'll stop back sometime when the shop's open. Thanks for the offer."

"Romy, I called the building…" Gracie starts talking with the woman. They close and lock the door behind me, and I stand on the street outside, fighting the urge to look behind me.

I shove aside the thought, spot a trash bin, and toss

the empty coffee cup inside. I check the time on my phone and stalk toward my SUV.

This afternoon was a nice distraction. I discovered a great coffee place, explored something on my bucket list, and killed a few hours while my kids spent their first day at their new daycare. Now it's time to put Gracie out of my mind and get back to reality.

Bright Start Daycare Center is anything but. When I arrive at 2:30, a half an hour early for afternoon pickup, I hear my daughter Cora's distinctive wail from the parking lot. I haul ass to the front door of the red brick building, careful not to slide inside my still-wet sneakers.

"Miss Thompson?" I holler into the security camera mounted over the front door. "It's Ryder Cooper."

A frazzled-looking college-aged girl unlocks the door and waves me in. "Hi, Mr. Cooper," she says, wiping loose strands of hair back into her messy pony-tail. "Cora hasn't had the best day."

"I hear." I try not to take out my frustrations on this kid because she's just an aide. She doesn't own the most highly recommended daycare center in Star Falls. Miss Thompson does, and that's the woman I want to see. *After* I see my children. "Where is she?"

The girl whose name I remember is Kellyn or Kelly, something wonky that starts with Kell... Or is it Keel?

Anyway, the girl nods and motions for me to follow her down the large central hallway.

As we pass each room, I see exactly what I'd expect in a daycare of this size. Kids and aides in various states of play. Some are eating snacks from colorful fabric lunch boxes; some are sleeping. A few of the older children color at small desks.

I see my son Luke's favorite blue-striped shirt as he hunches over a desk. He's by himself, not coloring, not reading...doing nothing. He's five years old and is taking the move to Star Falls as well as can be expected. He seemed excited to start day care, and both of our brief visits went well.

I figured the first full day I left the kids here would be tough, but not like this.

My heart tightens at the sight of my sweet, talkative son alone, seemingly looking at his hands. I can see two aides supervising the Beetles, which is the nickname given to this room. I'll find out why he seems so sad once I know Cora is all right.

My attention goes back to Kell-whatever.

"How long has she been screaming?" I ask loudly, hoping my voice isn't drowned out by the squeak of my shoes on the floor.

She looks back at me with a grimace. "Um, I think she's been pretty upset since lunch."

I check my phone. "Isn't lunch at 11:30?"

She nods. "Yeah. But Miss Thompson thought she'd settle down."

I rub my face hard, working the stubble on my face

between my fingertips while I try to control my emotions. My three-year-old child has been a hysterical mess for hours, and no one's called me? I square my shoulders and ready myself for confrontation.

I'm used to managing an entire football field full of rowdy teenagers. I can handle messy.

What I cannot handle is my baby crying. And clearly, Miss Thompson can't either.

When the aide reaches Miss Thompson's office, she taps lightly on the door. I can see Miss Thompson on her knees on the floor, patiently shaking a stuffed animal at Cora, while my daughter stands facing a wall with a window that overlooks the parking lot.

Cora's little hands are spread against the drywall, and I can hear through the door the hysterical shuddering of her breaths as she calls for me on every painful exhale.

"Move," I demand and pull open the door of Miss Thompson's office. "Sweetheart, I'm here. Daddy's here." I swoop down and pick up my daughter before she can even turn around. She immediately drops her head against my shoulder, snot and tears wetting my T-shirt.

She's babbling inconsolably.

I just stand there, rocking lightly in place, patting her back and her soft, dark hair. "Shh," I urge. "It's okay, sweetheart. Daddy's here." While I cuddle my daughter, I glare at Miss Thompson. She looks shocked and a little annoyed.

"Mr. Cooper," she says, scrambling to her feet. She's

young, probably just a few years out of college, and yet she's the executive director of this place.

When I interviewed with her before I enrolled my children here, she seemed to understand my situation. Now I am painfully aware that whether she understands my situation and whether she can handle my children are two very different things.

With the hand stroking Cora's back, I wave at the teacher to stop talking. "My children haven't been in anyone's care but family," I grit out. "We discussed at length what they've been through. What we've all been through."

Miss Thompson looks annoyed and yet also a little embarrassed. "Of course, I understand," she says, talking way too fast and way too loudly. I feel Cora jump in my arms at her tone. "Both Cora and Luke have been doing just fine."

"Just fine?" I echo. This is nothing close to fine. "My daughter has been in hysterics since lunchtime? What the hell happened?"

"I'll have to ask you to watch your language," Miss Thompson says primly.

I find my eyebrow lifting up in outrage. "I will speak however I want to speak around my own children," I say. "I'd like a refund for the balance of my deposit," I tell her. "I'm pulling my kids out of here." I turn on my very wet heel and squeak my way down the hallway.

"Mr. Cooper," Miss Thompson calls, trailing after

me as I head for Luke's classroom. "Please wait. This is against our safety protocols."

That has my anger boiling over. I turn to her with a glare that I hope is nearly as lethal as it feels. "Safety protocols? You have the nerve to throw safety in my face when you let my child sit in hysterics for how long now? Three hours?"

Miss Thompson firms her lips. "She saw Luke when the classrooms passed by each other over lunch," she explains. "She wanted her brother, but you know, as I explained, we do not allow children to play with children outside of their assigned age pods. It's a safety consideration."

I grip my daughter with both hands. Cora is completely quiet now, her snuffle-snorts absorbed by my shoulder as her tears ease. "You think keeping a three-year-old away from her brother when she's been through what these kids have been through…" I shake my head and turn away. "So you, what? Took her out of the classroom so she could be punished by screaming in your office with you?"

"It's policy, Mr. Cooper," she shouts in a shrill tone. "You were provided a copy of our policies when you enrolled your children."

I don't even bother to lower my voice or turn back to her as I shout, "Your policies are bullshit, lady!"

I turn the knob on the Beetles room and don't bother going in.

"Luke," I yell. "Come on, kiddo. We're going home."

The classroom aides look at me with their mouths open, but my son is already grabbing his backpack.

Shit.

I forgot about that. I'll need to get Cora's. But then I realize Luke's got both his and his sister's.

I bend down to greet him. "Hey, buddy." I clap a hand on his tiny shoulder and pull him to my waist. "How'd you get your sister's backpack?"

Luke looks near tears, and he doesn't answer right away. His lips tremble, and a tiny dribble of spit bubbles on his lower lip.

I shake my head, calming myself down so I can reassure him. When he gets nervous or stressed, he struggles to speak. It's something I've had checked out, and the pediatricians and child therapists have all assured me it's nothing more than an anxiety reaction. He talks up a damn storm when he's happy or angry. But when he's stressed or nervous, it's like he bottles up everything inside and he cannot get his words out. Like father, like son in that respect.

I push past the question.

It doesn't matter now.

I just want to get my kids out of here.

"It doesn't matter. You did great, okay? I'm proud of you for looking out for Cora."

He has their empty backpacks in his hands. Since they only brought their lunches and snacks, there's nothing left to tie us to this place. I let Luke hold on to the backpacks while I keep Cora in my arms, and together, we head for the front door. The small family that's been through so much, going through one more disappointment together.

"Mail me a refund, or I'll dispute the charges with my bank," I call behind me. "My kids aren't coming back."

CHAPTER 3
GRACIE

THE SMALL PLUMBING problem that forced Chloe's bookstore to close is *not* a small problem for my tattoo shop. As it turns out, The Body Shop needs time to dry out. That means remediation and remodeling. And all of that means the shop is closed and I'm losing income.

Thankfully, Chloe was able to tear up her carpet, dry out the bookstore, and bring in one of my brother's firefighter friends who does floors on the side to lay down some nice new strip flooring pretty quickly, and they were able to reopen in time for the weekend.

The last thing I want to do is sit home and stew, so around noon, I roll into downtown Star Falls, desperate for coffee and hoping against hope that I'm not too late for a peanut butter crisp.

I park my car on the street, because contractor trucks are taking up all the employee spots behind The Body

Shop, and fumble through the contents of my purse for loose change. I'm about to give up the hunt and stick my debit card into the meters when a reminder alert goes off on my phone.

"Ugh." I groan and almost drop the precious two quarters I just touched among the numerous tubes of ChapStick, used tissues, and crumpled receipts at the bottom of my bag. "As if I needed a reminder."

The day the shop flooded, I was supposed to call and schedule a doctor's appointment. In all honesty, I'm completely in denial that I need to make this call. Hell, I'm in denial that I need to go back to the doctor. The call is like that tiny first step on a path leading right into a nightmare. If I don't make the call, I don't have to take the step. Or so I keep telling myself.

But something inside me knows I need to get the stinkin' test. It's not a life-and-death health situation. I'm fine, mostly. I just…my stomach tightens even thinking about the mess that started last year. The incredibly hot but short-lived fling. The missed period. The calls and texts that went ignored until the last one. The one that broke my heart into a million pieces until, just a few weeks later, I lost the pregnancy.

Tears sting my eyes as I think about the hours I spent alone in my apartment, wondering if I should just call my mom and tell her everything, but decided against it.

In the year since all that went down, my doctor has begged me to come in for testing to see about future complications or even the viability of another pregnancy.

Part of me wants to sort it out. To know the truth so I can face it and move on with my life. That centered, determined part of me keeps the reminder to call the damn office and schedule the tests active on my phone.

The stronger part of me, though, keeps hitting snooze.

Day after day.

Hitting pause on that alarm makes me feel better and worse at the same time. I know the problem doesn't go away just because I ignore it. But it kind of does, you know?

I see a parking enforcement car pull up the block, so I'm forced to get out of the car before Marianne or Gordon, whoever's on duty today, gives me a ticket.

I snooze the notification on the touch screen and toss the phone back in my purse. I climb out of the car, feed the meter my two measly quarters, and squint into the beautiful sunshine to see how many minutes I've got. Fifty cents won't buy me much time, but it'll be more than enough to get my caffeine and cookies.

The bookstore is crowded with shoppers lingering with coffees in their hands and market bags over their shoulders. The store is warm and cozy, and the new flooring, a faux-wood laminate, looks surprisingly real and inviting.

I breathe in the familiar scent of fresh coffee and paper, my new favorite combination and fixation.

Paper flowers made from donated used books decorate the walls. There are comfy-looking chairs with well-loved pillows just begging to be rocked in. On the large-screen television mounted on the wall, the state poet laureate is reading from her latest book, her beautiful words scrolling by in bold captions.

I notice that the table display set up near the television looks nicely picked over. Meaning the shoppers have noticed the poet and bought her books. Chloe is so, so damn clever. Such a smart businesswoman. She's turned her aunt's failing café into a thriving, homey place.

I drop my purse at my feet and lean my elbows on the counter with a dramatic sigh.

"Extra-large?" Chloe's eyes sparkle as she takes my order.

"Heck yeah, and Chloe, please," I say, "tell me you're not sold out of peanut butter crisps yet."

The luster of her smile dulls a bit as she nibbles on the corner of her lower lip. "Oh Gracie, I sold out. The kids' event…" She waves her hand toward the gathering.

I shake my head. Just my luck, but hell, I can't really be mad. "Next time," I say. "I'll get here *before* story hour."

"Text me in the morning, and I'll set one aside for my favorite sister-in-law."

"I'm your only sister-in-law."

Chloe laughs, waving me off before she walks away.

As she heads to the back to make my coffee, the

woman reading in the middle of the circle motions me over.

Carol Miles is one of my mother's best and oldest friends. And by oldest, I mean Ma and her crew of ladies have been tight since, like, high school.

Carol recently separated from her husband, Earl, who owns the shop where my brother Franco works as a mechanic.

Small-town life is something else.

You can't sneeze without someone you know sending their blessings your way.

Carol is standing holding a colorful book, but by the looks of it, story hour just ended. Most of the parents and kids are wandering past the folding chairs toward the waist-high kid-friendly bookshelves. A brand-new lightbulb-shaped area rug rests on the new flooring, and a sign hand-lettered by Chloe reads, "Great Ideas Start th Play."

I steer clear of the kids' section and anything kid-related these days. And while I'm not exactly triggered being around kids, I still sort of go out of my way not to hang with them. There are times when seeing a baby clutching its mother's shoulder in line at the grocery store will bring me to tears. It's not a good look when I'm in line with people I don't know, but here at the bookstore... No, thanks.

I grab my purse and head over to greet Carol. I tiptoe between the folding chairs and lean forward to kiss both her cheeks.

"Gracie. You're a sight for sore eyes," she says a little

too loudly. "Your mother told me about the water damage at the shop."

"Thankfully, it's not that bad. The building owner wants to make sure we have all the permits and inspections in order before we reopen. Won't be long now," I assure her.

I live with my parents. Every night since the store closed, I've had to listen to my parents' worries about my finances. The last thing I need is one of my surrogate moms piling on the concern.

"Well, you know you can come help Bev at the shelter. She's always looking for volunteers."

Chloe approaches us with my coffee in her hands but looks rushed. "I have a customer at the register," she says. "Be right back to chat."

I ignore the way Carol is looking at me and get back to the matter at hand. "With all the fosters Ma brings home, our house is already like a shelter," I remind her.

"Ummm…Excuse me?"

We both lower our eyes to a little boy, maybe five or six years old, who is looking up at Carol. "Can you help me find a copy of the book you read for story hour? My dad can't find it."

The boy is pointing toward the shelves, when a muscled wall of a man ambles between the rows. I see a familiar set of broad shoulders and a sultry, warm smile.

"Coffee?" he calls out. "Is that you?"

I chuckle that he's not talking about my coffee. He's calling *me* Coffee.

"Hello, Kicks." The nickname rolls off my tongue and surprises me. It feels a little intimate, but I don't know his name, so I decide to just shake it off. I jerk a thumb toward the counter, trying not to spill my coffee. "Hate to break the news to you, but they sold out of peanut butter crisps."

"Guilty," he admits, giving me a full-teeth, panty-melting grin. I don't have time to react to the feelings his body and smile are giving me because he bends and scoops up a little girl who links her arms around his neck. "I think Cora and I here devoured every last crumb that Chloe gave us." He nods toward the front counter. "I'm on a first-name basis with the owner now. But I never did get your name."

As she looks from me to the stranger, Carol's cheeks are the same flaming magenta as her lip color. I can already tell she's on fire watching me chat up a hot stranger, but I hope she has the sense to realize this is not one of those matchmaker moments my ma's friends are so fond of orchestrating.

This man is a possible customer of the Body Shop and, by the looks of it, very, very attached.

"I'm Grace," I tell him. "But everyone calls me Gracie."

"Gracie, you haven't met Coach Cooper yet?" Carol hands the book she was holding to the little boy. "Allow me to properly introduce you."

Coach Cooper sets the little girl in his arms on her feet and extends a hand to me. "We sort of met but skipped the names part. I'm Ryder Cooper."

Stupidly sexy name for a stupidly sexy, attached, unavailable, I-can't-have-him man. But this is good. If I can't have him, I can't make any mistakes. I take his hand in mine and squeeze. "I'm Grace Bianchi."

"Gracie is a tremendously talented artist. She owns The Body Shop next door." Carol is oozing motherly charm and the kind of classic lack of subtlety that's practically a requirement for entry into my ma's lady friend group. "And Coach Cooper was just hired by Star Falls High…" She wrinkles her nose at him. "Remind me what you're teaching?"

"I am a coach, but I'm not coaching this year," he supplies. "Not officially." He trails off, and his pretty eyes gather shadows. "This will be my first year back at work after some time off, so I'm keeping my schedule as flexible as I can until these knuckleheads are in school full time."

He releases my hand and scoops the little girl back into his arm. "This is Cora," he says, his voice sweeter than Chloe's peanut butter crisps. "And my son, Luke. Can you two say hi?"

Cora is biting her lower lip and staring at me with eyes as sweet as her father's. Her cheeks are full, and she's got those tiny, perfect baby teeth.

"Hi, Cora," I say.

"Hi," Luke says. He's holding the book Carol gave him in one hand, and he gives me a tentative smile. He looks at his dad with a grave expression. "Dad…"

Ryder lowers himself, groaning audibly as his knee pops. He tightens his hold on his daughter as he rests first one knee then the other on the brand-new flooring. "What is it, buddy?"

Luke ducks his head but never takes his eyes off me. He mumbles something in his dad's ear, and Ryder chuckles. "You can ask her, buddy. Go ahead."

The little boy looks at me with eyes that look nothing like his father's. He must get those from his mom. He looks scared and his lips open like he wants to say something, but he just stands close to his dad, fisting the corner of Ryder's short-sleeved shirt.

I'm no baby whisperer, but I figure the best way to talk to anyone is to get on their level. I kneel on the floor and set my coffee and my big purse on the floor by my knees.

"Let me guess," I say, giving the kiddo my brightest smile. "Are you wondering about the pictures on my arms?"

Luke looks at his dad and then back at me with a tiny nod.

"I knew it." I clap my hands softly. "Okay, look here." I point with my right hand to the figures on my left arm. "Do you like animals?"

Little Luke nods, fully caught up in the moment. Even little Cora is watching, following where my finger is pointing.

"What does this look like to you?" I ask, tapping the colorful design on the top of my left forearm.

"A rabbit," Luke blurts out, looking very proud of himself. "Two rabbits?"

I nod. "You're right. A mama and a papa rabbit." I

figure that is a safe place to start, but then Luke steps closer to his dad.

"We don't have a mama anymore," he says. "Only my dad."

A fist tightens around my heart, and I flick a look at Ryder. There's something unreadable in his face, not grief or sadness, but something more resigned and weary. If these kids don't have a mama, I've probably trod on tender ground, but I figure the best way to smooth over the moment is to just keep going.

"Look here. Do you know what this is?" I angle my arm awkwardly but give the little boy a view of the inside of my left bicep.

"It's definitely a squirrel," Luke says confidently.

I nod. "Yep. And do you know why I have a squirrel and bunnies on my arm?"

Luke's eyes go wide. "No. Why?"

I can't help laughing then, and I point to my shoulder. "This is a tree," I explain, my fingers trailing over the intricate green leaves and branches. My entire left arm is covered shoulder to wrist with a woodland scene. I go back to the bunnies. "These two represent my parents…" I catch myself and don't say mama and papa again, just in case that hits a nerve. "And the squirrel represents my middle brother, Vito." I cup my hand to my mouth and lower my voice as though I don't want Vito to hear.

"He's always running around and eating everybody else's snacks," I explain.

Luke starts cracking up, and even little Cora chuckles. There's, of course, more meaning behind the animals I chose for my siblings, but I think this is plenty of information for now. I point out the owl that stands for my older brother.

"Because he's a really bossy know-it-all," I say, and I'm rewarded with yet another round of laughter when I roll my eyes. I save the best for last.

"And this…" I point to a frog wearing a crown that covers the entire top of my left wrist. The jaunty expression is made even more hilarious by the flippered foot that rests on the cap of a bright red-and-white polka-dotted mushroom. "This little guy represents my brother Benito. He thinks he's the king of the family." I lean closer to Luke and whisper loudly, "Benny's kind of a pain in the butt."

Luke now seems completely relaxed. He even leans forward and touches the crown on Benny's little frog head. "Did you draw all that?" he asks.

I shake my head. "I didn't draw it myself. I came up with all the ideas and had a very talented friend draw these. And look." I rub my fingers vigorously against my skin. "It doesn't come off. The colors are there forever."

Most kids who've never seen tattoos this detailed or this up close ask the same things. Does it wash off? Did you use markers? Why is it forever? I've become pretty good at predicting the questions, but then little Luke asks one that throws me.

"What about you?" He cocks his head and inspects the furled leaves and long, lush green grass that fill up the spaces between the animals that represent my family. "There are no more animals, so what happened to you?"

Ryder's voice is warm and invades me like a sudden ray of sunshine breaking through a storm. "Look, buddy. She's the tree."

Without touching me, he points to the front part of my shoulder, where a face has been carefully designed to blend in with the leaves. It's an elegant profile, but the dark brow that's been inked to look like part of a leaf's texture and the distinctive lips and nose are clearly mine.

"It's a family tree," Ryder says, a note of such deep respect in his voice that I feel raw. I'm used to people asking about my tattoos, complimenting them, even. But his appreciation seems so much more profound.

I nod, surprised at the sudden emotions clogging my chest. I stand up and smooth my hair, trying to calm my heart. I don't know why it's racing.

Or why the hell this man with his shoulders and his sneakers and his mama-less kids has my tummy in knots. But this feels like the right time to end this conversation. "Now you know all about my art," I say, trying to sound more cheerful than I feel.

Carol has been quietly watching the whole exchange like we're an episode of her favorite reality show.

I lift a brow at her, trying not to feel annoyed because I know if this man is single, the very next call she'll make will be to my mother. The unofficial Star Falls matchmaking circle doesn't need much to start spinning out of control. My ma and her friends have gotten their panties twisted over a whole lot less than a harmless chat between me and a guy who's new to town.

This means it's definitely time for me to go.

CHAPTER 4
RYDER

IT'S one thing to have a single tattoo that has some kind of personal meaning, but it's an entirely different story to permanently ink a family portrait of sorts onto your body.

I didn't look closely at her tattoos the other day, but now that I know what her left arm means, I want to know everything about this woman. She must be close to her family, and she clearly has a sense of humor. But more than that, she has depth.

I've caught glimpses of her other designs, and while she didn't walk my son through the images on her right arm, she has a whole sleeve there too that now has me incredibly curious.

I want to ask more, to say anything to stop her from walking away.

"Daddy, your tummy is talking." Cora takes my face in both hands and looks right into my eyes. "We didn't eat lunch yet."

I feel something sticky that I wish I could identify smearing from Cora's hands onto my face.

Gracie is doing that awkward thing where she's rocking on her heels, trying to slip away.

"Daddy, I'm hungry too." Cora's looking like she's about to burst into tears, so I have about two seconds to redirect her before she has a full-on meltdown.

"I'm sooooo hungry," I moan dramatically, amping up the silliness to keep my baby girl happy. "And Cora is sooooo hungry. Let's ask Luke. What about you, little man?"

Luke nods and echoes our enthusiasm as he rubs his belly. "Soooooo hungry."

"All right, let's find a place to eat lunch." I turn my attention to Carol, the lady who read the book at story hour. I specifically avoid looking at Gracie, who is still standing with us, watching the weirdo lengths that I will go to when I'm trying to calm my kids down with one of those perfect brows lifted high on her forehead. "Ms. Carol, it was great meeting you. Kids, can you thank Ms. Carol for the fantastic story?"

While my kids mumble thank-yous, Carol is squinting and opening and closing her mouth until, finally, she blurts out, "Benito's."

"Excuse me?"

"Gracie, why don't you take them to Benito's?" Carol rushes on.

Grace huffs an odd sigh and slings her big purse farther back over her shoulder. "Carol, I don't know if..."

"Is that a lunch place?" I ask, holding up a hand. "I don't want to impose. We're always in the mood for a drive-through food."

"Drive-through," Carol practically screams. "Coach, you're new to Star Falls. Have you eaten at Benito's Italian restaurant yet?" She peers down at Luke with a giant magenta smile that is so sincere it melts my heart.

This is what I expected of small-town living. One part meddlesome, one part enthusiastic, but completely backed by good intentions.

"Do you like pasta?" Carol asks the question like she's asking kids if they want a meal of cookies—breathless and filled with wonder.

Luke's eyes go huge, and I have to stifle a groan. Carol has said the magic word. All Luke ever wants to eat is pasta. I've probably gained ten pounds in carb weight since…well, since I've been cooking solo for these kids. "Pasta is my favorite." Luke is beaming. "With red sauce," he adds. "But I also love mac and cheese."

He's not showing any signs of shyness or anxiety. What the therapists have told me is to let my son lead the way. When he wants to talk, encourage it, but don't make a huge deal out of it. The fact that he's at ease in the bookstore, talking to these complete strangers, reassures me that the drama of the daycare hasn't set him back too much, if at all. Even if I would be fine with a cold sandwich or a kiddie meal, if Star Falls has a pasta place, I'm thrilled to take a recommendation.

"So, buddy, does that mean you want to try a new place for lunch?" I ask him.

"Please, Dad. Can we?" Luke grabs my free hand and swings it, and I crumple inside.

I'd move into Benito's and eat three pasta meals a day if it kept my son feeling happy and balanced. I look to Carol for reassurance. "Is it family-friendly?" I ask. "Cora still needs a booster seat."

Carol barks a laugh so sharp that Cora flinches in my arms. "Is it family-friendly?" she cackles.

Grace holds up a tattooed finger. "All you need to know about Benito's is right here." She points to the jaunty frog prince on her arm. "My brother owns the restaurant. I happen to know that the place is exceptionally family-friendly. If you want, I'll call ahead and let him know to give you a nice table on the terrace."

I'm about to tell her that's not necessary when Carol intervenes.

"Gracie, why don't you take Coach Cooper to lunch? He's new to town. He needs friends. You can be…his friend…"

The look on Grace's face almost has me bursting out laughing. She's huffing her cheeks and glaring, looking mortified and angry, and it's the sweetest and yet sexiest combination imaginable.

I brace for the full eyebrow fury, but to my surprise, she sighs and turns to me. "I don't know if your kids really want me crashing their lunch," she says. "But I didn't get a peanut butter crisp for breakfast, so I could eat."

"You eat cookies for breakfast?" Luke picks up on that immediately, and I'm about to set him straight, when Grace tries to walk back her misstep.

"No way," she tells him, bending slightly. "My...uh, dentist would freak out if I ate cookies for breakfast. But sometimes I skip breakfast, so I kind of think of the cookie as a lunch appetizer."

"A lunch appetizer..." I chuckle under my breath. Before the woman gives my kids any ideas about how to skirt the few rules I do enforce around mealtime, I go back to her question. "Luke, Cora, should we invite Grace to join us for lunch today and go to Benito's for pasta? Or would you rather have drive-through food in the car? Your choice."

I know my kids and I'm sure what Luke's going to say, but I figure Grace will feel more at ease hearing it from them.

"Pasta," Luke says, nodding. "And Grace. Please, Dad."

Cora tightens her arms around my neck and starts whining. "I'm thirsty, Daddy."

"That's close enough to a unanimous vote for me," I say, meeting Grace's eyes. "If you don't mind playing tour guide through the culinary wonders of Star Falls, that is."

"Dad, what is a..." Luke's about to press me for a definition of culinary, but Grace is chuckling and nodding her head.

"I'm in," she confirms.

"I'll explain culinary in the car," I tell Luke. "It's a

fancy word that means food." I slip my phone from my pocket, juggling Cora, and hand Grace the device. "Do you mind putting the address in my GPS app? I'm still learning my way around town."

She takes my phone and types in the address and then reaches to hand it back to me. After a moment's hesitation, she says, "Should I…" She looks down at the touchscreen. "Should I put my number in? Just in case you get lost or we get separated?"

My pulse thunders, and I can't explain the sudden lightness in my chest. She's offering me her number? Maybe it is only because she thinks I'm a distracted dad, but whatever her reasons, I don't hesitate to agree.

"That'd be great," I say, trying to downplay the rush of excitement that twists my belly.

It occurs to me then that it would be really rude if I didn't invite Carol to join us since, after all, it was her idea. "Miss Carol," I say, nodding at her, "are you a pasta fan? I'd hate to leave you out of this lunch adventure. Can you join us?"

The woman leaves no doubt about her intentions when she vigorously shakes her head. "Oh no," she says. "No, no, you two go. I've got to get home to make lunch for Earl." Her eyes gleam, and she vigorously waves both hands at us like she's shooing us on our way. "Enjoy, now. Gracie, make sure you call me later!"

Carol scurries off, leaving me alone with a very annoyed-looking Grace. But as soon as our eyes meet, she softens. "You'll get used to them," she says. "Small-town people are the best kind of people, but they will get all up in your business."

Before we're able to head out, Cora says, "Daddy, I have to go potty."

I don't have time to respond before Luke starts complaining. "Dad, I want pasta."

I take the situation in hand before things devolve.

"Okay, kids, listen up." I use my coach voice, trying to remember that I'm in a bookstore where people are reading and shopping. "First," I say loudly, "we find Cora a potty. Then, lunch. Everybody got it? We have a plan, right? Are we cool?"

Luke nods, and Cora wriggles in my arms, which means I need to find a restroom before both Cora and I need a change of clothes.

I turn to Grace. "We're going to be a few minutes. Meet you there?"

She nods. "Bathroom's right there." She points to a partially open door toward the back of the store.

I gather up my kids and give her a last look of thanks. I don't know what else to say because even though she's meeting us at the restaurant, walking away feels like I'm leaving something important behind.

By the time everyone has gone potty, me included, and I've made it to my truck, belted everyone in, and gotten settled, it's probably been a solid half hour. Wherever

Grace is, she's probably impatient and questioning whether we bailed.

Once I'm secure in the truck, I pull out my phone and start the mapping app so I know how to get to Benito's. Before I pull out of my parking spot, I search my contacts for Grace. I'm a little nervous when I can't find anything under Grace. I start at the letter A and scan quickly through the list, hoping she didn't change her mind and decide to bail. Then I see it.

A new contact, one I've never created. But the name she entered isn't Grace. It's Coffee.

I pull up the contact, check the GPS for a travel estimate, and type out a quick message.

Coffee, Kicks' crew is on the way. ETA seven minutes.

I hit send and have a response back before I even put the car in reverse. It's a whole message in just emojis—a little coffee cup, a sneaker, two baby faces, and a thumbs-up.

I chuckle and pull out of my parking spot, not at all surprised that a tattoo artist communicates with art. I can't help but think of all the delicious dirty texts someone like her might send, but then I stop myself.

This isn't a date. This is a meal. A kindness done by a woman who was harassed into joining me for lunch.

Grace isn't interested in me. She doesn't even know me, and I don't know her. The woman needs to eat, and how could she refuse Carol's none-too-subtle matchmaking? I'm sure she has no interest in a single father of two. I can't believe I'm even wondering if she might.

As I travel the blissfully traffic-free roads of Star

Falls, I let my mind wander to what kind of person a tattoo artist might want to date.

I can't explain the way Grace's boldness, her directness, and her colors draw me in, but as I park the truck in the parking lot of Benito's, I'm feeling excited. I'm looking forward to walking into that restaurant and seeing her dark locks and her expressive face.

I take a deep breath and turn to face the kids. "Who's hungry?" I bellow.

"Me!" Luke shouts back.

"Let me hear you, Cora. Are you hungry?"

"Hungry," she echoes.

A rush of emotion fills my chest. These are my kids. My family. Little people whose lives and hearts I'm responsible for, and yet I've taken them away from both sets of grandparents to start over in a small town. Away from the memories. Away from the only house they ever lived in. Away from the only place that connects them to memories of their mom.

As I unbuckle their seat belts and hold their hands to cross the lot, I say a prayer to Elizabeth to look out for us. To help me do right by our babies.

As if in answer, a bird swoops low as a flock plays some kind of game of bird tag, I duck my head to avoid being hit.

"Whoa." Luke points to the sky. "Dad, that was crazy. Those birds are playing!"

"I don't know if birds play, bud, but they were close, that's for sure. I'm just glad I didn't get bird poop in my hair. Anyone want to check?"

Cora squeals and says, "Ewww, poop in your hair."

I pick her up and remind her of all the poop of hers I've cleaned over the years. I've got my daughter in my arms and Luke holding my hand when I look up and see a set of serious black brows staring at me through the plate glass window that faces the parking lot.

She's here. She really did wait.

As I approach the front, I can see that Benito's is a really cute place. Lush plants and colorful flowers bloom in real planters outside. The chairs out front look like a ragtag assortment of real lawn chairs someone's grandmother might have at a summer cottage.

The vibe is inviting and warm. It's exactly the kind of family-style place where I'd expect to get an amazing meal in a relaxed environment.

My hands are full, so Grace pushes open the door for us.

"Thank you, Coffee," I say, nudging Luke to go on inside.

"You're welcome, Kicks. Glad you made it." She steps aside while I carry Cora indoors.

The inside of Benito's is even more inviting than the outside. I smell garlic and bread and tomato sauce, and a happy buzz of chatter rises from the full tables.

Grace leads me to the hostess stand where a woman who must be close to eighty is adjusting a pair of reading glasses on a beaded chain around her neck. Her stylish ear-length bob is pure white, which makes a sharp contrast to the shocking red lipstick she wears.

She's got thin brows that arch deep and fake nails that are ornamented with something sparkly on top.

Gracie goes behind the hostess stand and loops an arm around the woman's shoulder. She plants a loud smooch on the hostess's cheek. "Rita, these are my lunch dates."

The woman lets her glasses flop from her hand to her chest. She looks from me to Cora, back to me, then to Gracie before clasping her hands together in front of her chest.

"Get out of here," she crows.

That's literally the last thing I expect this cute old lady to say, but before I can react, she comes bustling around the hostess stand, headed right for me.

She holds out both hands, and I'm not sure if I should hold them, kiss them, or hand over my baby. I opt to take one hand awkwardly and shake it.

"I'm Ryder Cooper, ma'am," I say.

"Ma'am." The hostess looks back at Grace and crows. "The manners on this one! I like him. Kind eyes, Gracie, and a hell of a body." She looks back at me and shrugs. "Pardon my language in front of the kiddos." She points to Cora and then Luke. "Rita just said a bad word, but you two didn't hear a thing. Am I right?"

Cora giggles and buries her face in my shoulder.

I decide to redirect before this conversation gets out of control. "Cora, Luke, can you say hello to Ms. Rita?"

While the kids chat up Ms. Rita, Grace grabs two large, plastic-coated menus and two paper kids' menus, along with two cups of crayons. She holds up the cups and lifts her brows as if asking whether the kids can have them, and I nod.

"All right, Rita, we've got to get these kids some food." Grace sets a hand on the hostess's shoulder and holds up the menus, grabbing an extra kids' menu to draw on. "I'll seat us," she offers. "I marked out table twenty on the terrace."

"I'll have that cute college boy bring over a booster seat," Rita says. "Have a great date, you two."

"It's not… Oh, never mind." Grace shakes her head and looks me in the eye. "I guess I did call you all my lunch dates."

"I don't mind that at all," I say, a lot more growl in my voice than I intend.

Grace looks at me and flushes a bit, but then heads off through the crowded restaurant, leading us to a terrace.

A young kid dressed in black jeans and a white button-down shirt carries a booster seat in one hand and looks from Grace to me like he's completely lost about what to do with it.

Grace thanks him and points to where she wants the seat, and then she waits while I settle Cora and help Luke into a chair. I start to pull out the chair between the two kids and then stop.

"Is this okay?" I ask. "I feel like I should pull your chair out for you."

She grabs the back of the wooden chair and drags it across the smooth wood flooring.

"No…I mean, yes. This is great. I'll sit here. It's not

really a date," she clarifies. "I mean, not that you'd have to do the chair thing even if it were."

She drops into the chair, and I sit. And then it's just the four of us.

Two strangers across the table from one another with my kids. At her brother's restaurant. It freaks me out even to think it, but this feels familiar. Easy. Almost too easy. Like family.

I'm not sure I believe in signs, but I'll take all of this as an omen of good things to come.

CHAPTER 5
GRACE

THE SECOND WE SIT DOWN, I set a kids' menu and a paper cup filled with crayons in front of Cora. Ryder takes one of the menus and the second cup, then holds up an extra menu.

"Did you want this?" he asks, grinning wide.

I can't help the massive, goofy smile that takes over my face. "Yeah," I tell him, then turn to Cora. "Can I borrow a few crayons from you? I promise to share."

Cora is a seriously cute kid. She's got light brown curly hair that just reaches her chin. She has a perfect set of baby teeth, and when she smiles, every one of them is on full display.

"Here," she says, holding the whole cup out to me. Her hand shakes a little, and I take the cup gently so the whole mess of colors doesn't spill on the floor.

"Thank you." I look over the rounded, dull points and scowl. "This sucks." I flick a look at Ryder. "Pardon my language." I make a mental note to watch what I say around the kids. It's been a while since I've been around kids this age. Probably since I babysat in the neighborhood for cash in high school. I don't see the need to censor myself normally, but with kids, I should probably set a little bit of an example.

I hold up a red with an unacceptably flat tip. It's like somebody dropped and snapped the end off and then tried to chew their way through the crayon. I grimace and stick the thing back in the cup. "We need a crayon sharpener or something. Hang on."

I turn around to dig in the purse on the back of my chair and turn back at Ryder's sexy chuckle. "What?"

"If you have a crayon sharpener in that purse, I might just have to marry you."

If the words surprise me, they look like they shock him.

"Inappropriate. I'm sorry. I'm going to stuff my face with bread and look at the menu," he says before I have a chance to say anything.

I twist my lips into a grin and grab the phone from my purse. I punch in a text message, and a few moments later, Rita comes walking toward the table with two brand-new boxes of crayons in her hands.

"Let me see those," she says, peering down the end of her nose.

I hand her a cup of crayons and shake my head. "You tell my brother if I have to come in here and sharpen the crayons, I'm charging him my hourly rate plus."

Rita cackles. "You do that, Gracie." She takes the cup

from me and the second one from Luke, and then leaves us with two brand-new, unopened boxes.

I crack open a pack and breathe the familiar, waxy scent. I pull out a soft shade of salmon pink and admire the sharp tip. "Hmm," I sigh. "Now that's bliss. Nothing beats a brand-new crayon." I return the pink to the box and hand it to Cora.

While she dumps every single color onto the table in front of her, I tuck her chair closer to the end of the table and bend over to grab two strays that have fallen to the floor.

Then I lift up the kids' menu in front of me. "Luke," I call out. "See this?"

I point to a piece of pasta drawn in a cartoon style, complete with a bow tie, big eyes, and a happy smile.

Little Luke nods.

"I drew the whole thing," I tell him proudly. "Look here." I point to a tiny squiggle in the lower right corner of the menu. "That's my name. Grace Bianchi."

Luke's wide eyes would be adorable, but the way his mouth drops as though I just told him I could fly makes me positively glow.

"No way." He grabs the menu and looks at every piece of food and every character I've made. "You drew this?"

I nod proudly. "My brother asked me to design the kids' menu, so that's what I did. Take a look."

Ryder holds one end of the menu and reads the food choices out loud to Luke. "Cora," he says. "They have grilled cheese. Do you want grilled cheese or pasta?"

"Grilled cheese," she says without looking up. Her little head is bent over, and she's dutifully coloring the eyes on Mr. Mostaccioli red.

"I respect your bold colors," I tell her, tapping my finger on the menu.

Just then, a different college-aged kid comes by with two tall plastic glasses of ice water for Ryder and me.

"Hi, Grace," he says. "Can I bring drinks for the kids?"

"Do you have anything kid-safe?" Ryder asks. "I left my little one's sippy cup in the car."

"Dad, it's not a sippy cup. Cora isn't a baby." Luke sounds annoyed in a very protective older brother way. He reminds me of Franco when we were young, and it melts away a layer of ice I hadn't even realized was frozen around my heart.

"Right. Sorry, buddy." Ryder ruffles the boy's hair and then orders organic apple juice pouches and one glass of water for the kids to share.

"I know what I'm having," I say, borrowing a crayon from Cora. "Do you want a recommendation?"

Ryder nods. "If it's good enough for the sister of the chef, yeah. Please."

I flip open the adult menu and point. "The wood-fired pizzas are the best you'll ever eat." I bring my fingertips together and blow a kiss. "Mmmm. So good. But my favorite dish is the ravioli."

I'm looking Ryder right in the eyes when he says, "I trust you."

There's a moment when we stare each other down, and neither one of us looks away.

I hear Luke scribbling on his menu and Cora peeling the wrapper from a crayon she just snapped in half. But I can't look away from Ryder. His beautiful eyes. His sexy grin. And the way he stares at me as though he very much likes what he sees.

He runs a hand through his hair and blinks. I think he's going to look away, but he doesn't. We stare and stare, my heartbeat thundering in my chest and a buzz of excitement competing with the hunger pangs in my belly.

He's hot. He's exactly my type. But he's a *dad*.

I give in and let him win, snapping my gaze away and focusing on my kiddie menu. I use the black crayon I borrowed from Cora to sketch two whimsical birds in flight.

Todd returns with the juice, and Ryder places the orders for the kids—grilled cheese for Cora and pasta with meatballs for Luke.

"I'll have the ravioli," Ryder says.

I glance up and give him an approving nod, but it's like his eyes never left my face. His stare is intense, and there's something real that passes between us. Something charged and exciting.

Nope, I think. *Absolutely not.*

"Make that two," I tell Todd, then immediately busy myself drawing.

The man is hot, yes. But he's got two kids. He's new

to Star Falls. And *because* he's exactly the type I normally am attracted to, he's bound to be a mess.

Even as I think the words, I am not sure I want to believe them. He's an attentive dad. He seems to know his kids really well and to be a really hands-on father. Maybe he's a total user or a cheat. I run through the list of every shitty thing every well-built, athletic, clean-cut guy I've ever dated has done. This Ryder guy… I mean, damn. Even his name is sexy.

He's no different from any of them, I remind myself, pressing the wax even harder into the menu paper.

He wants one thing from a woman.

And when he gets it, he'll be gone.

I know how this would go if I gave in to the flirtatious little dance we seem to have going on. I'd have sex with him. It'd be great because, look at him. I mean, my mouth has been watering since long before we came to the restaurant. We'd have a few weeks of fun, and the minute I started to get attached, the excuses would start.

They are all the same. Guys like Ryder. Men in general.

I have three brothers. I know the best that men can be, and I know they are self-righteous, immature, selfish, and every other shitty thing on the planet. Too bad this one is so incredibly freaking hot.

I focus on finishing the birds and sipping my ice water, until Ryder finally says something.

"Wait…are you drawing those birds? The two from

outside?" He's staring across the table, peering at my work.

"Yeah."

"I swear they were trying to attack me when we got out of the car." Ryder reaches a hand across the table. "Can I see that?"

I hand him my menu and then lean over to inspect Cora's work. "I love that," I tell her, pointing to the flaming-pink hair on the Lady Meatball. "You know what I like to do? Can I show you something?"

Cora nods, and I reach over and open my hand for a crayon. "Give me any two colors," I say, "doesn't matter which ones."

Cora hands me turquoise and orange. I nod appreciatively. "These are going to go really well together. Look."

I pick the tube-shaped character made out of ziti. She hasn't colored it all in yet, so I use the turquoise to make gently curved lines that follow the shape of the ziti's body. Then I make small round polka dots with the orange. "Another color," I say, holding my palm up for more.

Cora hands me green and pink, and I color in around the orange circles with the pink, then draw large flares spiraling out from the pasta body in green.

"See?" I say, handing her back the paper. "You don't just have to fill in the lines. You can make anything your mind can imagine. Patterns inside the lines, emphasis outside. You can add anything. You just need a little inspiration and a few colors."

"What's inspiration?" Luke asks. He's busy drawing a railroad track on the bottom of his menu.

"That right there." I jab my finger in the air excitedly. "Look at that. I would never have thought to put a train with pasta people, but how cool is that? You were *inspired* by an idea to do something different."

Luke blushes and hands me his menu. "Will you inspire something on mine?"

I smirk and take his menu. "Only if you inspire something on mine."

Ryder is still looking at the birds I drew. I made two very classic, old-school tattoo-style swallows. Not at all the birds from the parking lot, but it doesn't matter if they are exactly what I saw. These are, I guess, inspired by the doves or whatever they were flying in tandem.

Ryder stares at my artwork, a little tightness around his lips. "Your birds are really, really stunning," he says. "I might have to come back for a tattoo after all."

"What?" Luke gasps and stares at his dad with wonder. "You'd get a tattoo, Dad? All over your arm?"

Ryder holds up a hand and shakes his head. "We'll see. I was just complimenting Grace's skill."

The kids and I color in silence until I hear something that stops my heart in my chest.

"Gracie?"

"Oh God." I literally drop the crayon and cover my face with both hands. "Brace yourself," I mutter.

"Sorry?" Ryder looks confused, but before I can explain, I leap out of my seat.

Rita is leading none other than my mother and her friend Bev over to our table.

"Lookie here." Rita looks incredibly proud of herself, and under normal circumstances, I'd be thrilled to run into my mom on a random outing. But seeing her like this is literally my worst nightmare. I'm going to have to do a lot of damage control.

"Hey, Ma," I say, clasping her in a hug and kissing both cheeks. When I move on from my mom and kiss Bev, I can see my mom's face is so damn red, it nearly matches her store-bought hair color.

Then before my mom can say anything embarrassing, I turn to Ryder. "Ryder, this is..."

But I'm way, way too late to stop the embarrassment train. It's like Luke's picture, except my mom is the conductor and she is revving the engine and aiming right for Ryder.

"I'm Lucia Bianchi," Ma says, holding out her hand to Ryder. "I'm so sorry. I had no idea Gracie was on a date."

"Ma," I snap. "It's not a date. Ryder's new to town, and..." I sigh and clamp my lips together. I could be reciting the nuclear codes from memory, and my mother would be completely oblivious. She only has eyes for the man she thinks her daughter is on a date with.

Ryder takes my mother's hand, but then she draws him in for a huge hug.

If the hug bothers Ryder, he definitely doesn't show it. He hugs her back and seems like an old pro at making mom small talk. He introduces the kids one at a time, having them say their names and how old they are.

"Luke, you're five years old. Such a beautiful boy, you are." Lucia coos over his gorgeous kids just like she coos over everything. Enthusiasm overload. It's actually really cute, and Luke seems happy with the attention, at least.

"I'm almost six," Luke clarifies. "I'm in first grade."

"Will be," Ryder corrects. "Luke starts Star Falls Elementary in a couple weeks."

"We have very good public schools here in Star Falls." Then Ma turns her attention to Cora. "And who are you, sweetheart?" Ma bends over, her necklace dangling like a tiny sparkly windchime.

Cora points to it but doesn't touch it. "I like your necklace," she says in the sweetest, shyest toddler voice ever.

My mother full-on flushes, and I swear, if she could have done it without getting arrested, she would have scooped Cora up and taken her home.

"You know my Gracie is an artist," Ma says proudly.

Luke looks confused. "You're her mom?"

"Yes, I am. Gracie is my youngest, but she's all grown up now. I have three sons as well, but Grace is my only girl. My baby." My mom lights up, and for a minute, I feel the pride and love she feels for me.

My mom introduces the kids to one of her best friends, Bev, who runs the local animal shelter, and then drops the bomb I should have known was coming.

"So, what brings you to town, Ryder? Did you and your wife relocate for work?"

I want to slap my forehead at the brutally obvious question, but Ryder's answer deflates my anger before it can even gather steam.

"I'm a widower," he says simply. "We lost her not long after Cora was born. I took some time off to raise the kids, but now that they are a little older, we're making a fresh start. I'll be teaching part time at Star Falls High this fall, with plans to ease into coaching when I can put Cora in all-day kindergarten."

That information lands hard. Ma's affection can feel like a spotlight—harsh and direct sometimes—but if you see it for what she intends it to be, it's just pure. Like sunshine she can't contain. It pours out of her and spills onto anyone who cares to listen. Beside Luke and Cora, who are growing up without their mother, Lucia's purity, her passion for her kids, suddenly feels like a blessing I've taken for granted.

I look Ryder over curiously. I didn't know he was a widower, but how would I? I know virtually nothing about him, so anything I might have assumed about his life is just my attempt to put together a story to keep myself safe.

I have such a terrible track record with men. I'm questioning every look and every word that have passed between us. Is he a lonely single dad looking for love? A hookup? A mama for these little kids?

Aw, hell no. I promised after what happened last year, I would not—I repeat, *not*—rush into anything.

Not sex. Not a relationship. Not even a date. That's not what this is, and if he had any confusion about that whatsoever, I'll set his ass straight.

For her part, my mom doesn't miss a beat. She clutches a hand to her chest and shakes her head. "I'm so sorry for your loss," she says, genuine tears sparkling in her eyes. She lowers her voice and steps closer to Ryder. "No one should experience something like that so young." She looks at Cora and Luke, and again, I'm thankful Ma doesn't pick up both kids and march them to her house.

If she had her way, she'd probably stuff them with treats and love and play surrogate grandma for as long as Ryder would allow it.

But instead, she firms her lips and reaches up a hand to cup Ryder's cheek.

He looks stunned at first, because who wouldn't?

Can you cut it with the touching, Ma? She and I are really going to have to have a talk later about boundaries.

But he looks at me, and I shrug and shake my head like I'm washing my hands of the ticker tape parade that is Lucia. He seems to relax, though, and sort of leans in as if giving her permission to manhandle him.

"Ryder—and this goes for you and your children—any friend of Gracie's is *family*," she says emphatically. "Anything you need—babysitters, recommendations for doctors, homemade dinners—you call me. You come to any one of us."

She motions with her free hand toward Bev. "Any of

us, you hear? That's what small-town living means. All for one, and one for all. Isn't that what they say? In fact, Gracie—" she turns to me with a glare "—why haven't you invited Ryder over for dinner yet?"

I don't even bother trying to explain myself. When Ma goes on a rant, there's nothing that can stop her. Maybe my dad, but not always. So, I just sigh and watch while Ma practically inducts Ryder into the Bianchi family. She's a one-woman welcome wagon.

He looks overwhelmed and a little flustered, but seeing him listen to my mom, his stubbled cheek in her hand, is strangely satisfying. He seems like he's actually listening to her, which is endearing. Sweet. He's got a grateful smile and the faintest hint of a blush reddening his cheeks.

I'm honestly a little jealous it's so easy for Ma to touch the guy.

She releases his face, and I expect him to brush her off or politely decline all of her offers, but to my absolute shock, he accepts.

"We'd love a little help," he says. "I actually just pulled my kids out of Miss Thompson's daycare, and I haven't made much progress finding alternative arrangements. If you had any suggest—"

Ma cuts him off with a dramatic hand gesture at her friend Bev. "What did I tell you? Did I not tell you?"

Ma shakes her head, moving her body so much with the gesture that her jangly bracelets clang together as she moves. "That woman is a mess. I know Kelly's mother and that whole family… Nothing but drama."

"Ma." I butt in, putting a stop to small-town gossip. "Kelly runs a fine place. If it didn't work out for Ryder, it didn't work out."

"Miss Thompson's name is Kelly? I thought her summer aide was Kelly?" Ryder looks even more confused.

Thankfully, Todd is coming our way with a tray heavily loaded with food.

"Ma, our food's coming," I say, lifting my brows to dismiss her. "We can continue this another time."

"Oh, all right. All right, I'll leave you to your meal." She grips Ryder's arm and gives it a visible squeeze. "We'll talk later, sweetie. Grace will give you the details about dinner. Enjoy your date."

She gives him such a bright smile that I don't even have the heart to correct her. The fact that he's a widower doesn't make this a date. It wasn't a date before I knew he didn't have an ex-wife hanging around. For all I know, he has a girlfriend or a side squeeze. And on top of it, if he's a widower, the man is a full-time dad.

But correcting her won't discourage my mother. Not now that she's got the idea in her head. I'm going to be hearing about this not-a-date date later. I'm damned sure of that.

Ryder grins at my mom, and it's like the temperature on the already hot terrace goes up ten degrees. He's so sincere. So sweet. And yet there's nothing sweet about the way he looks at me after he calls out, "Nice to meet you, Mrs. Bianchi." His toothy smile and those chocolate-brown eyes look me over in a way that's positively brazen.

Ma tuts for a minute about him calling her Lucia before Bev has to physically take Ma by the elbow and end the world's longest goodbye. By the time poor Todd has managed to get our plates on the table, I'm glaring with my entire face.

"Goodbye, Ma," I warn.

"My Benny's the best chef in Star Falls. Enjoy."

Ma teeters off on her heels, but they aren't going far. Rita seats Lucia and Bev at a table literally ten feet away.

Great.

"You're not from a small town?" I ask.

I watch while Ryder comes around to cut Cora's grilled cheese triangles into four smaller triangles. He squirts a little line of ketchup on the plate for her to dip her fries and then two small dollops to make a smiley face out of ketchup.

She laughs and says, "I'm going to eat the eyes first."

"Savage," Ryder teases, then kisses his daughter on the hair. Once he sits, he looks directly at me and answers my question. "We moved from Columbus," he explains. "We had a condo downtown. City folk through and through."

I nod, lifting a brow and sighing. "Well, good luck. It may take some getting used to, living in a place like Star Falls. The people are the best you'll ever know, but…" I motion my hand back toward my mom. "They will get right up in your business. And I mean, right up in there."

Ryder laughs and rubs his chin as if remembering my mom grabbing his face. "I haven't been grandma-bombed in a while," he says. "I can't say I minded one bit."

I unroll the paper napkin from around my silverware. "Grandma-bomb," I repeat, unable to shake the warmth that fills my chest. He's so…sweet. "Just don't go giving her any encouragement, or she'll order wedding invitations and start looking at venues."

Ryder's grinning, but he has no idea how serious I am. My mother's mission is to make sure her kids are happy, and that includes being happily partnered. If she didn't spend so much time volunteering and hanging out with her lady friends, marrying off Benny, Vito, and me—now that Franco has Chloe—would be her full-time job.

"So, what do you think, bud?" Ryder nods at Luke, who hasn't said a word since his lunch was delivered.

"This is the best ever," Luke says through a very full mouth. "Like, my new favorite, Dad."

"That's good, but try to chew and swallow before you talk next time." Ryder smiles, making even the correction seem loving. Then he looks at me, a fork poised over his plate. "So, this smells amazing."

I spear a single ravioli and smile. "Tastes even better."

Cora drops a fry on the front of her shirt and leaves a massive ketchup streak on the pale pink top she's wearing. She picks up the fry from where it fell between her legs and sticks it back into her mouth.

"Oh," I say, a little grossed out, a little impressed. "Should I get, like, a wet wipe or something?" I ask, pointing to the stain.

Ryder shakes his head. "Did anybody really eat if there's no visible proof on the front of at least one shirt?"

I chuckle and watch Ryder. He widens his eyes, chews, then rubs his face with a hand. "That might literally be the best thing I've ever eaten in my life," he says. "What's in it?"

I nod, then take a bite of my own, letting the meatball mixture inside the ravioli linger on my tongue. "Spinach, pork, beef, and three types of cheese. Super freakin' good, right?"

Ryder watches as I eat, licking the remnants of sauce from my lips. "Super freakin' amazing," he agrees.

Within a few seconds of our finishing eating, my brother hustles up to the table wearing a long-sleeved double-breasted chef's jacket embroidered with his name.

"Hey, Gracie. I didn't know you were coming for lunch. You should've texted." He leans over and kisses my cheek, then extends a hand to Ryder. "Nice to meet you, man. I'm Benito Bianchi."

Ryder introduces himself, standing and pumping Benny's hand vigorously. "Pleasure to meet you. I was just telling your sister this may be the best thing I've ever eaten."

Benny's grin is sly, and he points at me. "Get your phone and record that," he says. "I want bragging rights with Pops."

I shove my brother away. "Your ego's big enough. Let us eat before your personality ruins the meal." I stick out my tongue at him playfully, which makes both Luke and Cora laugh.

"Hey." Benny points at the kids. "Can I send over a little something for after the meal? Any dietary no-no's here?"

My brother has owned a family-style restaurant long enough to be a master at discreetly asking if he can send over some dessert for the kids. No faster way to annoy a customer than to offer something the parents don't want or don't allow.

"Anything's fine," Ryder says. "Thanks again, man. Absolutely delicious."

Before he leaves, Benny bends down and stage-whispers in a voice so loud, I'm sure the whole terrace hears him. "Enjoy your lunch *date,* little sis."

I shake my head, mindful of the fact that if I smack him, I'm setting a bad example for Luke and Cora.

I'm just about to take a sip of water when I feel a hot set of eyes boring into me. I peek over at my mom, and she waves like a child, all giddy and big smiles.

I groan and drop my face into my hand. "Welcome to Star Falls."

CHAPTER 6
RYDER

AFTER I TUCK the kids into bed for the night, I settle in front of the TV and fall asleep. I don't mean to, but it's a habit I can't seem to break. Every morning I set my alarm, so I have at least an hour before either of them wakes up. It may seem like a small thing, but getting a first cup of coffee and a shower with minimal interruptions is a major indulgence.

Not that I don't love having little kids. I love those two more than anything in the world. I wouldn't change a thing about being Luke and Cora's dad. Except, of course, being a single parent. Doing this without a partner. My wife. Their mother. Complete shitshow.

The time flickers across the screen, reminding me in black-and-white that it's nearly nine. I massage the crick out of my neck before checking Cora on the baby monitor. She's far too old to need it anymore, but I set it up after we moved to Star Falls while she got used to a new room.

I think it made us both feel better at first. I'll wean us off the device in a few weeks, but for now, I can peek in on her and be confident that she's safely asleep in her big-girl bed. And she can feel good knowing that the room is new, the house is new, but she only needs to open her eyes and look at the little camera to know Daddy's right there. Like I always have been. And always will be.

I roll my shoulders and debate what to do. It's too late to start a movie, but I really don't have the energy to throw in laundry or unload the dishwasher. I grab my phone and figure I'll check the sports scores on some of the apps I follow, when I see I have three missed texts.

One's from Elizabeth's mom:

Send more pics of the kids when you have time, Ryder. Tell them Grandma loves them.

Back home, Elizabeth's parents lived in a suburb of Columbus and would watch the kids every once in a while to give me a break. I knew leaving the circle of friends and what little family we had close by would be an adjustment, but Rebecca and Daniel were surprisingly supportive of this move. As much as they love their grandkids, Rebecca is managing partner of a law firm and has no plans to retire. Daniel's a senior vice president at a place he's worked at since he graduated college after serving in the Air Force.

Neither one of them is the kind of grandparent to

spend hands-on time with the kids. And that's not a bad thing. To be honest, it's made moving away easier. There was so little left back in Columbus to hold on to.

I sigh and make a note to send Grandma Rebecca some of the pics of the kids getting settled in Star Falls. Her message came in around seven when I was putting the kids to bed, so she probably knew better than to expect a text back tonight.

The next message is from my buddy Austin, the one good thing I miss from Columbus.

What'd I tell ya, bro. You see the news about Goodwin?

Austin is single and will most definitely be up at this hour. It's Saturday night, so he's probably not sitting at home on his phone, but I drop him a message back anyway.

Missed the news. What about Goodwin?

Austin is a sports fanatic. He's one of the guys who was never good enough to play past high school. But he's got a mind for stats.

Austin was the one friend who stayed close after Elizabeth died.

After I reply to Austin, I read the third text I missed. It's the oldest one, the one that arrived sometime between when I gave the kids baths and brushed their teeth. I hardly register the name of the sender when I open the message and see a load of emojis.

Sorry about my family today. They're a lot, but they mean well.

Gracie's message is followed by an angry face emoji,

a sweary face, and then at least five mind-blowing emojis.

My pulse quickens, and I drop back down on the couch. What are the odds she's even home right now? A woman like that's probably on a date or out with friends. The same things I'd probably be doing if I were single.

I debate for a bit whether I should text her back. What should I say? It means something that she texted me first, right? Could she be interested?

Rather than question myself anymore, I pull up her message and reply back.

Your family was great. Lunch was great. Now I know about the best coffee and the best lunch in Star Falls. What other best of's am I missing out on?

I hesitate before hitting send. Does that sound too flirty? Too forward? I don't want to sound like a dick who's asking her to keep playing tour guide.

"Fuck." I delete it and start over.

Your family is great. Lunch was great. You are great.

"Oh, sweet fuck, no. I can't send that."

Delete. Delete.

I get up off the couch and start pacing, annoyed with myself that I'm literally breaking into a cold sweat over a stupid basic text.

Loved meeting your family. Thanks for the "best of" tour of Star Falls. Any chance you can hook me up with the best sneaker store in town?

Nope, nope, nope. The sneaker thing is done and dusted. Time to put the tired joke in the bin. I delete the whole thing and nearly toss my phone on the floor. But then, I get an idea. I punch out the message, then read it over:

Your family seems great. I'm planning on eating at least five meals a week at Benito's. But next time, I'm bringing a crayon sharpener. I don't think I'll have as much pull with the hostess if you're not with me.

I think that one over a bit, then add an emoji of a crayon, which I swear I had no idea was even an option before I looked for it.

As I click send, even my hands are starting to sweat. I feel like a kid who can't believe his crush is actually texting him.

Before I can stress myself out further, I get a reply:

ravioli, peanut butter crisps, crayon emojis. Life-changing week.

I chuckle and wish I could see her face. Maybe I should call her. Is that weird? Would she answer? Instead, I go the neutral route.

Was your mom serious about helping me find childcare?

I click send before I can second-guess myself. But the moment the text leaves my drafts, I know it was the wrong thing to say.

"Shit. I went right into dad mode."

I rub my eyebrows and mumble, "Way to shut things down fast, asshole."

Was my mom serious? You might want to leave a spare key under the mat for her. That way, she doesn't have to bother you when she drops by unannounced to meddle in your business.

That message has no emoijs in it, but she follows it up with a second text of a girl with dark hair shrugging and another one of a yellow face laughing.

I start to feel the tiniest glimmer of relief, and I say so.

Very cool. I could use a meddling mom-type in my life. Especially if that means I'm free to let you take me out again.

I click send and wait, watching my phone for a reply, but nothing comes. *Annnnd shit.* What I thought was clever and flirty was probably just...not.

I'd ask her out in a hot second. I don't know how I'd get time alone with her without some sort of childcare, but Grace is gorgeous and funny. She seems so at ease with my kids. I don't know if a woman like her would have any interest in me, let alone any man with kids, but I don't have long to fixate on my worries. My phone rings a second later.

"Hey, I know it's late. You got dad stuff to do?" Her voice is sultry and quiet, like maybe she's lying in bed.

"No, uh, no," I stammer, jumping up from the couch and pacing the living room again. "Kids are sound asleep, and I did all the dad stuff."

"Good." I can hear rustling as she adjusts the phone. "I'm watching a movie in bed. Thought it would be easier to talk. You have a lot to learn about living in a small town." She chuckles, and I walk to the kitchen to pour myself something to drink.

"Enlighten me," I say, holding the phone with one hand. "And if you hear that in the background, I swear

I'm pouring a glass of water. I did not take you into the bathroom with me."

She laughs, a loud, surprisingly sweet sound that sends chills down my spine. "I have three brothers," she says. "Not much would surprise me. But I might be a little less inclined to go on that date with you if you took me to piss on our first phone call."

"Ah," I say, grabbing the glass and heading back to the couch. "So, a date isn't totally off the table."

She groans. "Keep this up, and my mom's going to have us married off by Christmas. She loves to meddle in her kids' lives, in case you couldn't tell."

"I can appreciate a mom like that," I say. The words come out a lot quieter than I intended, and Grace grows serious.

"I'm sorry," she says. "I feel like I need to say that. You lost your wife. The mother of your kids. And they are so, so little. I'm close to my entire family, even if sometimes they feel way too damn close. It just feels weird to not talk about what you've been through. Is it weird for you?"

"With you, no. Can I be completely honest?"

"No, lie to me, Ryder." Gracie snorts, and I picture one of those brows putting me in my place. "Seriously," she says, growing more somber. "Tell me anything. You don't know me, but I'm a very trustworthy person. Even though Star Falls is practically fueled by gossip, I prefer to keep private shit private."

There's something else in her voice when she says that. Almost a note of sadness. I'm sure she's been on the receiving end of small-town talk at some point. She's probably speaking from experience.

"Well, I'm probably making the buildup a lot more serious than it needs to be," I say. "I have dated a little bit since Elizabeth passed, but I didn't tell any of those women that I was a widower."

"What?" she squawks, and I hear rustling sounds like she's sitting up in bed. "So, what did you do? Like, make up crazy stories when they asked?"

I laugh. "Nothing quite that exciting. It's not like I told them she ran off to join the circus or anything like that."

"Who even does that?" she challenges. "Nobody joins the circus anymore. Aren't they, like, unethical? You need to come up with a better story. Really make them wonder."

I laugh again. "I'm shit at this."

I realize that makes me sound insecure, and I try to backpedal fast. Fuck, I'm not cool. I tell myself to calm down. She's just a woman. A beautiful, tattooed, spunky woman who called me. I just have to talk to her.

"Most of the time, when it came up, it was enough to say that we weren't together anymore, and I had full custody of my kids. Most women were either turned off or turned on by that."

"Yup. Exploding ovaries," she murmurs. "It's a real thing. A hot guy with two cute kids. I can just see the dating profile bio."

I can't let that one go. After I put visions of me next to Keanu Reeves in her head, I'm soaring at the compliment. "Hot guy?" I grin and push ahead before she can answer and break my heart. I don't think I want to hear it if she really wasn't flirting with me. "So, what about you? Ever try the online thing?"

I'm more than curious about her life. I want to ask everything. I want to know it all.

"I tried the online thing when I was younger," she says.

"Younger. How old are you?" I ask.

"Thirty-one," she says. "I tried a couple apps in my twenties, but every single guy either wanted a free tattoo or thought someone who looked like me just wanted to hook up."

"Damn," I say, trying to lighten the mood. She sounds pissed, and I can't say I blame her. "Well, since I am not even sure I want a tattoo and I have no hope of bringing you into my bed unless you mind sharing it with a pile of plush toys, I think you're safe with me."

The words come out so fast, but I regret them even faster.

"So, if you don't want a tattoo, why did you come in the shop?"

"It's funny," I admit. "I've always wanted a tattoo, but I just never knew exactly what I wanted. Which is completely the opposite of who I am. I'm a coach by training, a teacher. I'm a rules guy. I like to know the rules of the game and then play by them. I color in the lines. I don't usually second-guess myself."

Except when it comes to beautiful women who feel totally out of my league.

"Wait. Did it drive you crazy today when I drew all over the menu? I color inside the lines when it matters, but if I'm playing? The whole world is my canvas."

My heart catches in my chest when she says that. That's something I already feel about her. Her freedom. Her passion. Her immediate honesty and sincerity that can feel almost brash. She's a big personality whom I could get swept up in and love every second of the ride.

"Your creativity is amazing," I tell her. "But I don't mean that in a 'hook me up with a free tattoo' kind of way. I loved that you showed Cora she didn't just have to color in the lines. That kind of freedom is inspiring. It's not something that comes naturally to me."

She's quiet, and I can't tell if what I've said is a good thing or a bad thing.

"So, if you weren't sure you wanted a tattoo, why again did you come into The Body Shop?" she asks.

I sigh. "New town, fresh start… I don't know. I've never actually been in a tattoo shop. I thought I'd go inside, check it out, and get the whole idea out of my system for good. I sort of did want one, I just…I don't know."

She laughs. "Oh, Ryder. That's rarely how it works. Tattoos are like snacks. You can never eat just one. Once you have a taste, it's an addiction."

"Addiction?" I echo. "That sounds dangerous."

"Fuck no," she says. "We only have so much skin, and most people only have so much money and time to devote. If you find a good artist, they won't let you get shit ink. Once you see something that is so beautiful and meaningful that it inspires you every time you look at it… I don't know. Plain skin just feels incomplete."

I can't imagine a woman like her ever feeling incomplete. I lean back against the couch and flick a look at the baby monitor to see Cora still sound asleep. I tug a blanket over my legs and settle in. "So, tell me about it. What do you like about what you do?"

"Well, I can't speak for all artists. There are a lot of trace jockeys out there who will put a French fry and burgers on the chest of a drunk kid for the right price. But most of us are artists. The body is just the canvas, you know? Each person is so unique, and each piece tells some kind of story. When I ink someone, I want to know the vision my client has. Not just for the one piece I'm doing, but any future pieces they think they might get. I ask about their plans, because if someone has a lot of real estate to cover and they put a giant turtle with googly eyes on their calf, that's going to be hard to fit into a bigger piece or even cover up later. I like to know the story behind why my clients want their design, so that if the piece won't work exactly the way they think it will, I can suggest options that maybe tell the story even better."

I'm intrigued by that and really curious. "So, your arm, for example. Did you have the whole design planned when you started it?"

She barks a harsh laugh. "Oh hell, no. I learned by screwing stuff up. I had a bunch of janky shit I let my friends do when we were learning. The tree is a cover-up that I designed once I got established."

"It's beautiful," I tell her. "It suits you."

She's really quiet when I say that, and I hope I haven't misstepped.

"I think you're beautiful. And I promise that's not just my way of getting free tattoo advice."

She giggles, and it's that sultry, sexy voice with a note of sweetness in it that reaches through the phone and grips my heart in a fist.

"Are you flirting with me, Ryder? You really don't have to try too hard. My mother's friends are probably firing up the matchmaking bat signal right now. You don't know the power of a small-town mom when she thinks she's found someone for her kid."

"Your mom didn't find me," I clarify. "We found each other."

That seems to take the conversation in a more serious direction than I intended, but I don't care. I'm interested in this woman. She texted me first. And I know all too well that life is unpredictable and short. It'll tear your fucking heart out and leave you with nothing left. It's up to us to fill up the spaces in our soul, so that when the tough times happen, we aren't alone.

"Gracie," I say, "I'm a single dad. A widower. I have some baggage, to put it mildly. But I would love to take you to breakfast tomorrow. Well, my kids and I would like to take you to breakfast. As soon as I can find someone I trust to help with Cora and Luke, I'd like to take you on a real date."

She's quiet again, and I wait. Maybe I pushed too

far. Maybe I'm too forward. But I'd rather know now and focus on being her friend if that's all she's up for. This is exactly what I wanted, running off to Star Falls. Someplace different. New friends. People who might truly care about me and my kids. People in my life who don't just want me to send pictures of the kids they can look at from far away.

The work of starting over didn't just happen the day after we lost Elizabeth. I have to work to rebuild a life for myself and my kids every minute of every day.

I need a partner who will be there day in and day out to live the reality with me. Maybe it won't be the first gorgeous woman I set eyes on in this town, but hell if Gracie isn't a start.

Is it crazy to already be thinking about the happy ending? Yeah, it is.

Do I give a single fuck? Absolutely not.

I'll never know what a better life might look like if I don't color outside the lines once in a while. So, I ask again.

"Meet us for breakfast until I can ask you on a proper date?"

"I don't get it," she says, a smirk I can clearly hear coming through the phone. "I thought we'd already had a real date? Are you saying lunch at Benito's didn't count?"

I laugh, but she's saying yes. She's going to meet me.

We're doing this.

"I want pancakes smothered in syrup," I tell her.

"Crisp bacon. Coffee as close to the bookstore's as we can find at a sit-down place."

She tells me about a couple diners and sit-down places, and we finally settle on Eddi's Eatery.

"It's in a strip mall, but if you like breakfasts, there's no better place. The food is fantastic and fast. Eddi with two D's and one I. You want me to punch the address into your GPS?" she offers, her voice a sensual tease.

"Are you offering to come over and do that now?" I growl, finally feeling the flirtation between us flowing again.

"If you leave a key under the mat for my mom, I might just take it first," she says.

We chat for a few minutes about what time to meet. By the time we hang up, I have half an erection and a whole-ass smile on my face.

It may be a family date, but I've got a date with Grace Bianchi.

CHAPTER 7
GRACIE

BREAKFAST WITH RYDER and the kids is nothing like our lunch yesterday. To start, Cora is an irritable mess from the moment Ryder stumbles through the parking lot with her in his arms.

"Bad night's sleep," he explains, his cheeks flushed. "Might be a rocky breakfast."

While we wait to be called for a table, Ryder paces the parking lot, doing his best to distract Cora. I keep track of Luke, talking to him about the bees that buzz around the potted lavender plants and asking about his favorite breakfast food.

All the while, I trade flirtatious smiles and longing looks with Ryder. Even though I am excited to see him, and he seems really glad to be here, it is hard to maintain our vibe from last night while he is bouncing a fussy three-year-old in his arms.

When we finally are seated at a booth, the waitress forgets to bring us a booster seat. When we finally flag her down to remind her, she says they are all out of them, so Cora ends up sitting in Ryder's lap.

The final shoe drops when an entire tray stacked with dirty dishes falls to the floor in an ear-splitting crash near our table. That sends Cora into a meltdown-level crying fit, thereby putting a glorious end to what has already been a difficult breakfast.

I shove the last bite of my Belgian waffle into my mouth while Ryder stares at what remains of his three-egg scramble.

"I'm sorry. We'd better go." Ryder picks up Cora and motions for me to meet him at the cashier. We reach the front counter, where a line of people are impatiently waiting to pay. He hands me his wallet.

"Can you pull out the red one? That's my debit card."

I don't even bother arguing with him over who is going to pay the bill. He has more than enough on his hands at the moment. I take the card and, when it's our turn, hand it over.

After the completely bored-looking woman rings up our order, I grab Ryder's debit card back and scribble his signature.

"Thanks," he says, his face tight.

"No problem," I reassure him, wishing I could be more help as I put his card back in his wallet.

I follow Ryder to his truck, not sure if he'll want my help getting the kids settled. I don't really know what to do. The entire morning has been off. And not just because the kids were fussy. I think, honestly, part of what's off is me.

I am interested in this guy. I like the patient way he talks to his daughter, the way he seems as helpless as I feel to ease her discomfort. He never once yelled or snapped. He is upbeat, positive, and involved. Nothing like the men I've known. Nothing like the last man who couldn't even be bothered to text me back even after everything that happened between us.

There's no doubt I'm starting to like Ryder already. But that just makes me feel all the worse. I don't know where or how I could fit into his life. The kids are a lot. I'm a lot. I am sure all of that combined will be too much for him. I've been too much for so many people, and those were people who weren't trying to raise two little ones alone.

Out in the crowded parking lot, I pull my sunglasses from my bag and give him a small wave as I turn to head toward my car.

"Gracie," Ryder calls, his voice finally sounding strained. "Can you wait a second?"

His cheeks are bright red from the heat and the exertion of juggling the kids. But his eyes search my face with a look so hopeful, it breaks my heart.

"Yeah. Do you want a hand?"

He shakes his head. "Just give me a sec."

I shift my weight from one foot to the other and fan the summer air, heavy with humidity.

Once he's fastened Cora and Luke into their child safety seats, Ryder pulls out his phone and plays a loud video. Some cartoon I've never heard of with a catchy beat on the device, which he hands to Luke. Then he leaves both rear doors open to keep the air flowing into the car.

Then he turns to me, reaches for my hand, and steps close to me.

"I am so sorry," he says. "This is nothing like what I'd hoped today would be. I want to make this up to you, Grace," he says. "I probably should have canceled this morning, but I really..."

He stops and leans closer. I can smell the heat mixing with the faint fragrance of his cologne.

"I just really wanted to see you," he says, his chocolate-brown eyes meeting mine. "I'm sorry if that was selfish."

I smile and shake my head, gripping his hand tighter. "It's fine," I say.

But to be honest, I'm not sure what more to say. Getting close to a guy like this is complicated, and not just because he has kids. Because he's everything I want. Because he has everything I've ever wanted.

Seeing what I want and getting it are two entirely different things. Just feeling how much this man draws me in makes me all the more certain I need to pull away before one of us gets hurt.

I stroke the light dusting of hair on his knuckles with one hand. "I hope Cora feels better," I say. "Is there anything I can do?"

"Gracie." Ryder's voice saying my name feels as intimate as a kiss. As caring. As insistent. It's like he can read the doubts as if they are written all over my face. "You don't have to *do* anything. I just want time with you. Time to get to know you. But if this is too much..." His grasp loosens on my hands, but instinctively I hold him tighter. "It doesn't make you a bad person." He waves toward the car, where the music from the video fills the air. "This isn't for everybody. I get that."

"It's not too much," I assure him, but I'm lying. "It's not about you or the kids. I just...I don't know what to do here. I'm not sure I fit or how to help."

"You fit because I want you to fit," he says, his eyes narrowing and his lips parting. "Come to dinner tonight. My place. We can watch a movie and talk after I get the kids to bed."

I shake my head. "I can't. I have dinner at my parents' tonight."

Ryder looks down at our hands. He laces his fingers through mine. "Do you want to see me again?" His voice is low, rocky. "Ever?"

I don't answer right away, even though I know that I do. I wish I didn't. I wish I could stop myself from leaning into something that I know can only lead to heartache.

I try to talk myself out of this. I hardly know him. Now is the time to shut things down. Walk away and chalk this up to a funny chance encounter. I clamp my lips shut, try to stop the words from coming out. And I almost do it. I almost release his hands, head straight to my car, and leave all this behind.

But then he lifts his eyes to mine. He grins, and it's

the cutest, sweetest, most endearing look he gives me as he mouths the words. "Please, Grace. Give me one more chance."

The gesture steals the air from my lungs. My eyes flutter closed, and all I feel is a rush of desire, of longing, flooding my limbs. He is sexy, sweet, powerful, and gentle all at once. I wish I were strong enough to run right now, but I'm not. I can't.

"Can I come by after dinner?" I blurt. "It's not that I don't want to be around the kids. If they're still up, we can all hang out together. But…"

He curls a hand under my chin, lowers his lips to my ear, and whispers, "Of course."

He lightly nuzzles my hair with his nose. A moment that passes so fast, the only way I'm sure it's happened is the racing of my heart that remains when he steps away.

"I'm going to try to salvage the day," he says. "Naps for everyone." He gives me a smile and then leans into the back seat to retrieve his phone from Luke.

"Say goodbye to Grace, kids," he calls out.

"Bye," Cora pouts, looking like she's about to start wailing again. Poor thing.

Luke waves vigorously while Ryder taps away at his phone, and then he slides into the driver's seat. He hasn't even turned on the car when my phone buzzes with an incoming text.

I dig through my bag, swipe the touchscreen, and grin. I have a text from Ryder. It's his street address with an emoji of a house and a little clock with the message, *can't wait.*

They pull away, and I get into my car. I roll down the windows to let in some fresh air, then grip the steering wheel while I lower my head to rest on my outstretched arms.

This is either going to be the start of something amazing—or my most epic heartbreak yet.

"Yo, sis. How's the boyfriend?"

By the time Benny makes an appearance at my parents', the rest of us are already seated at the table. Chloe and Franco are next to each other on one side. Vito and I sit on the other with our chairs pulled close to each other so there's room for Benny.

"Shut your stupid face," I tell him. "We're all waiting to eat."

"Gracie." My dad peers at me over the rim of his new eyeglasses. He scrubs a hand through his long waves of gray hair and shakes his head. "Your brother's face *is* stupid," he says, giving me a smirk. "That's not what I'm upset about. But what is this about a boyfriend? Why am I always the last to know?"

I shake my head and mutter, "I don't have a boyfriend, Dad. It's nothing. Can we drop it?"

"Pass the wine," Vito says. "And spill the details on this non-boyfriend boyfriend."

"Could we please talk about something else?" I grumble, grabbing the bottle of wine and pouring myself just a couple of sips since I'm planning to go to

Ryder's after, and I want to be clearheaded. Not only for the drive, but for the time we'll spend together.

"When is The Body Shop going to open?" Franco asks.

I shrug my response.

"Honey, you know if you need something to do until you get the shop back open, we can always use a helping hand at the shelter." Ma sets a huge salad on the table and rests a hand on my shoulder. "Now, let's talk about the real news of the week. Doesn't your father look dashing in his new glasses?"

My pops groans, and my brothers start teasing him. Chloe stares adoringly at Franco, and I'm just relieved that everyone is consumed with catching up and digging in.

Before long, Benito is on his feet, kissing cheeks, and rushing back to the restaurant. "Love you all. Great meal, Ma and Pops."

Once Benny leaves, Vito's next, making his excuses and heading downstairs to bed.

"I think your brother is depressed," Mom says in a hushed voice.

"Vito?" Dad looks concerned. "He'll be fine. Don't worry about him so much."

There have been some problems at the firehouse this year, and Vito's hours have been cut way back. He's applied to other stations, but for now, he's basically working part time. Not at all the career path he'd planned for when he went into firefighting.

Franco and Chloe help clear the dishes from the table, and I follow them into the kitchen.

"I'll do these," I tell them. "You two go relax or go do whatever lovebird stuff you all do. Go for a sunset ride or something."

My brother is a mechanic and treasures his motorcycles. The one he rode here tonight he restored with his own hands not long after he and Chloe moved in together.

Franco gives me a look. "You sure? You never volunteer for dishwashing duty."

"You're such a liar." I swat him with a dish towel and kiss Chloe on the cheek. "Go. Love you both."

Once they're gone, I lose myself in washing the dishes, but quickly, my mind drifts to Ryder, and then goes even further back.

I start to think about Levi.

Leviticus Olson. The worst mistake I ever made. The last guy I dated. It's been over a year since we broke up… God, if you can even call it that. We didn't even really date—at least not as far as he's concerned. A fling, a hookup—that's what it really was. A couple weeks-long flirtation that ended in a colossal ghosting.

I wonder if Ryder's ever ghosted anyone. If he'd do what Levi did. My cheeks burn with shame at the memories. Just thinking about it is enough to send me back to my room to swear off men forever.

"Sweetheart?" I feel Ma's hand on my shoulder, and I sigh.

"I got this. Go have a drink in the yard with Pops. It's a beautiful night."

"I know it's a beautiful night." Ma strokes my hair with a hand, scratching her nails lightly against my back. "I want to spend time with my baby girl. Is that okay?"

I nod and turn on the faucet, letting hot water wash away the suds I've made. "Yeah," I say softly. "Of course, it's okay."

Ma stands beside me and takes a towel. She dries the glass dish and sets it on the counter. I can smell her distinctive perfume, and I'm overcome with emotion.

This is my world.

My mother.

My home.

I can't imagine what life is like for Cora and Luke. Not having a mother. Not having a big family always around.

Yes, sometimes we're all way too close for comfort. But I've been so loved my entire life. I've never gone a day without talking to my mom, texting her a hundred times even though we live under the same roof. I can't imagine a life where I didn't have Lucia Bianchi as my North Star. Can't imagine never knowing her as a person, as an adult with a personality and interests and plans.

"You've been awfully quiet tonight." My mom clangs a cabinet door that's loose on its hinge as she puts away the dry dish. She curses under her breath, a mom-style curse. "Shiitake mushrooms. I've asked Vito ten times to repair that door. You'd think the man could find the time to squirt a little lube on it and find a screwdriver or something. Sometimes I don't know about that brother of yours."

"They're all idiots," I say.

"Yes," Ma laughs, "but they're our idiots."

It's an inside joke we've shared since I was a teenager, the youngest of four and the only girl.

We keep washing dishes until they're all done and the sun streaks pink through the kitchen window.

"Lucia!" Dad shouts from the living room. "Should I turn off the air? It's supposed to cool down tonight."

My mom lifts a brow and shouts back. "Your call, babe!" Then she turns to me and kisses me on the cheek. She grows serious and pets my hair. I close my eyes and savor her soothing touch.

"You know you can talk to me about anything, right? Anything, Gracie."

I swallow back the guilt and the shame. Maybe now is the time. Get this off my chest. Explain what really happened and what might happen next.

"I... Ma, I..."

"Lucia. Grab the wine and come outside. This sunset's going to be gorgeous."

My mom doesn't seem to want to leave me. It's like she senses I'm close to opening up. She cups my cheek with a hand. "You want to come watch the sunset?" she asks. "I bought new citronella candles. Maybe we won't get eaten alive by mosquitos this time."

I shake my head. "I'm good, Mom. I'm going to run out for a bit."

She looks like she's going to ask where I'm going, but then she stops herself. She looks me square in the eyes and just smiles. "I love you, sweet girl. And I'm proud of you. You know that, right?"

I wrap my arms around my mom and hold her close.

I do know. I know I'm loved. I know I matter. I have always been able to rely on the strength of my family. Why, then, is it so hard to forgive myself for what happened?

CHAPTER 8
RYDER

LUKE IS PLAYING with his toy train inside the bathroom as I hunch over the tub, giving Cora a bath.

"Dad, your phone." He grabs my phone, holding it out to me as he sits down on the toilet lid.

I'm on my knees on a folded-over bath towel, trying to wash Cora's hair without getting the suds in her eyes.

"Okay, bud," I say. "I'll check it in one second."

I smooth Cora's hair into a pile on top of her head and lean my face close to hers. "Listen, baby," I say, "you've got a pile of teeny tiny baby chipmunks wrapped up in your hair. If you hold very, very still, they won't fall into the water. Can you hold your head level so they don't get wet?"

This is one of Cora's favorite games. If she's in the mood to play, I've got about ninety seconds before she forgets and starts moving around so much the shampoo bubbles drip into her face.

"Munk?" she squeals, because chipmunks is a word she hasn't quite mastered yet.

"Yes, now hold still." I wipe my hands on the bath towel and check the message. It's from Gracie.

You really did leave a key under the mat! But I'm not letting myself in... That seems forward, even for me.

A smile spreads across my face as I quickly punch in a reply.

I'm elbows-deep in bathwater. You'll be doing me a favor if you let yourself in. Grab something to drink, make yourself at home. I'll be down ASAP.

I set the phone on the bathroom vanity and grab the cup I've used to rinse Cora's hair since she was an infant.

While she covers her eyes with her hands, I rinse out the shampoo, miraculously not getting any in her eyes.

I make quick work of getting her out of the tub, getting her into her pajamas, and brushing her hair.

Our bedtime routine after the bath usually takes a solid half hour, but with Grace downstairs, I need to give her a heads-up about story time and our usual routine.

I race down the stairs, finding Grace standing in front of the bookshelf behind the couch, thumbing through a photo album. It's marked Memories, and she's smiling as she flips the pages.

"Hey," I say. "Sorry I took so long." I'm so excited to see her, I hardly register what I look like. The front of my T-shirt is soaked, and the knees of my threadbare gray sweatpants are too.

She looks up at me, then looks me over from head to toe.

I walk up to her and shake my head. She's wearing a sleeveless black tank top that's all flowy and low-cut, exposing a sensual bit of cleavage. Tonight, she has on pink jeans that would look positively girly if they weren't intentionally shredded and frayed. She's barefoot, her black wedge sandals resting by the front door. Her hair is loose and soft, the black wings of liner around her eyes in stark contrast to the rest of her face which looks dewy and clean. No bold makeup, no lipstick. Just her.

"You look stunning. I'm so glad I dressed up just for you," I say, trying to make a joke out of how seriously inadequate I feel next to her.

"Are you fucking with me?" She gives me a grimace. "You make loungewear look stupid good."

"Is that a good thing?" I hesitate a minute, but then I open my arms, and she comes in for a hug.

She lifts up on her toes and whispers against my ear. "That's a very good thing," she says.

I growl a little and hold her close but then quickly release her. "Bedtime normally takes a while," I say. "Can you give me maybe thirty minutes? Make yourself at home. Dig through my drawers, eat my food…"

She pats her belly. "I ate with my parents, remember? But I will stalk your paperwork. Make copies of your social security number. Stuff like that."

"Excellent," I say, not caring what she does, as long

as she stays. "Every strong relationship starts with identity theft or some other felony."

"Is identity theft a felony?" she asks, lifting a brow. "I might be in more trouble than I thought."

I chuckle and motion toward the kitchen. "I have wine and beer if you want an adult beverage. Raid the cabinets for glassware. Only the butterfly and kitten cups are off-limits. Those are just for me. I don't share well."

She twists her lips into a smirk and waves me off. "Go on, then. I have snooping to do."

I dash back up the stairs and start with Cora. I read her a book, answer at least ten unnecessary questions, turn on her white noise machine, and check the monitor camera before I give her a bunch of kisses. Luke is wide awake and playing on the floor of his room when I get to him.

"Bud," I say, clapping my hands. "Bedtime, sleepyhead."

"I'm not tired." He looks at me and then yawns a long, drawn-out, dramatic yawn.

"Really?" I ask. "I had no idea you weren't tired."

I pick him up and sling him over my shoulder, making sure I've anchored my weight on my good knee.

Luke giggles, and I check the time on my phone. Twenty minutes. Grace has been alone downstairs for about twenty minutes.

"Buddy," I tell him. "Tonight, we need to pick a short book, or you can ask me five questions."

"Five?" he echoes and rubs his chin like he's seriously weighing his options. "How about ten?"

I shake my head. "It's too late. We have a big day tomorrow. We need to find a new daycare for you two chuckleheads." I ruffle his hair. "Dad's got a job to go to, and unless you're old enough to babysit yourself and your sister..."

Luke sighs loudly. "Five questions."

After giving him answers to five questions I never would've thought of in a million years, I turn the tables on him.

"Buddy," I tell Luke, tapping him on the nose. "I have a question for you now. Would you like to join a class? What would you like to do for fun with other kids? Soccer or gymnastics?"

Luke opens his eyes wide. "Anything?" he asks.

I nod.

"Can we go to a pool?" He asks it so immediately and so completely that my heart twists. Swimming in the pool at the condo where Elizabeth and I lived was just about the only thing Elizabeth could do with Luke when he was little.

"Do you remember swimming with your mom?" I ask.

He nods. "I loved splashing. I don't really remember Mom, though."

"You know what does remember her?" I tap his chest. "Your heart. She's always there, buddy, even when your brain is filled with so many new things you don't think you remember her." I stroke his hair and kiss his forehead. "Get a good night's sleep, and I promise, I will find a pool tomorrow."

I turn on the night-light, flip off the wall switch, and dash down the hall to my bedroom. I peel off the damp sweats and T-shirt, throw on my most comfortable jeans and a short-sleeved button-down shirt. Not a job interview kind of button-down, but what I hope looks like a date shirt, a comfy blue chambray. Then I head into my bathroom, roll on a refresh of deodorant, brush my teeth, and spritz the tiniest bit of cologne.

When I get to the living room, Grace is sitting on my couch. Her feet are curled up beneath her. She has poured two small glasses of red wine and two glasses of ice water. Both are on the coffee table. She's thumbing through another album of photos.

"I feel like I need to give you some kind of award for most patient woman alive. You waited forty minutes for me. I'm so sorry."

"Don't apologize. You're worth the wait." She pats the couch next to her and lifts one of those dark brows at me.

I sit beside her, not sure how close I should get, but wanting to be so much closer than this. Now that she's here, in my space, it's like I can't see anything else.

I am fascinated by her bare lips, the sharp ridges I want to run my tongue over on her top lip and feel each peak. I drag my eyes away from her lips and look down, but even the tops of her feet are tattooed. I could look at this woman forever and never grow bored.

"I am so glad you're here," I tell her. "I'm so glad you stayed."

She cocks her chin at me, her full lips twisting into a grin. "I'm glad to be here. Now I have questions." She scoots closer to me. She points to the wineglasses. "The bottle was open and fresh, so I assume you drink red?"

I nod. "I'm not a big drinker, so anything is fine. The water is perfect, but I won't let the wine go to waste either."

"Good." She lines herself up beside me so our thighs touch. She has two photo albums and opens one to a page she's clearly looked at a couple of times. "Who's this?" she asks.

"My wife's mother, Rebecca. You can tell by the scowl she's a lawyer."

Grace laughs and points to a woman in a wheelchair. "And this?"

"My sister, Allison," I explain. "Cora is named after her. My sister Allison is also a lawyer, oddly enough, but she has no connection to my wife's mom."

"I'm glad I decided against stealing your identity while I waited for you," she says. "Too many lawyerly types in the family."

I laugh. "You won't get Allison to come after you. She's a high-powered LA entertainment attorney. She does weird stuff. Intellectual property, contracts, stuff like that. And she hates leaving the West Coast. She insists, even though we were born and raised in Ohio, that she's allergic to rain."

"Can I ask about the wheelchair?" she asks. "I mean,

I guess I just did. I don't want to be insensitive, though."

"Nah, nah. It's fine. Allison would prefer people just ask and be open about their questions. It's like when people stare at your tattoos. I'm sure you'd rather them just say something than look at you funny and leave you both feeling weird."

"True," she says. "True."

"Allison was hit while she was crossing a street on foot. She was in college at the time, and so was the driver. The kid who hit her didn't have insurance on the car, and his parents had nothing. No money, no assets. Allison had always wanted to be a lawyer, so after she got through the recovery and rehab, she picked up right where she left off and went on to become the Elle Woods she always wanted to be."

Grace smiles. "That's awesome. Are you two close?" She asks the question gently.

I shake my head. "Allison has always been super independent, even before the accident. She is my half-sister. My mom married three times but only had two kids. We have different dads, and there's an eight-year age gap between us. She's a super-supportive older sister, but…" I shrug. "We lead very different lives. I became a high school teacher and stayed close to home. She doesn't visit often, but we video chat once a month so she can see my kids."

"I can't imagine not being close to my family," she says. She flips to another page in the photo album. "I still live at home with my parents and one of my brothers. I moved out for a short time but ended up deciding to come back."

She grows quiet, and I wonder what happened to make her move home. She looks like she's about to open up, so I wait and let her share what she wants. But then she pivots.

"My family is huge," she says. "Cousins and second cousins. My parents both come from big families, so reunions and weddings and stuff are jam-packed with people."

I lean back against the couch and loop my arm over the back of the cushions.

Grace looks up at me and gives me that brow. "Are you trying to cozy up to me, Ryder? Are you making a move?"

I am sure I blush eight shades of red. "I've been dying to touch you since you came through that door."

Grace gives a hilarious little huff and scoots closer to me, tucking herself under my arm. "I'll allow it," she says playfully. "So where are your parents now? And your wife's parents? Did you move to Star Falls alone?" She looks up at me and shrugs. "Sorry if I sound like a journalist. I just want to know your story. All the details."

"Okay," I say. "I was born in a little house outside of Columbus..." I'm teasing her. I'm not really going to tell her my life story from the beginning, but as I talk, I stroke the ends of her hair. My arm is over her shoulder so I can easily reach the soft strands. When I touch her, she presses her head back against my arm and breathes deeply. I smell lavender and something sharper, but I don't know what it is. "Grace," I murmur, lowering my face to her ear. "You smell freakin' amazing."

She rests a hand on my knee and squeezes. "So do you," she says. "Good enough to eat." She tips her head against my chest and stabs a finger against the photo album. "Stories first. Making out later."

"Making out?" I echo. "Will there be making out?"

"I think I'm owed, don't you?" She lifts her face to mine, her full lips pursed into a smirk.

"Do we have to wait?" I lower my face to hers and press a kiss against her forehead.

She looks at me, and her eyes sparkle. "Ryder," she breathes. "If I start kissing you now, I won't want to talk anymore."

I swallow and lift my head after taking one long, delicious breath. Her hair, if it's even possible, smells even better up close. I stroke the silky strands between my fingers but then pull away, trying to put maybe an inch of distance between us. Even though I really don't want to.

I groan. "All right," I tell her, scooting away just a bit. "You want my life story, you'll get it. But before you leave tonight..."

Since I've shifted my weight, her hand moves from my knee, but she manages to reach the muscles of my left thigh. "Keep going. Before I leave tonight, what?"

Her touch is gentle but firm. She kneads the tight muscles of my leg with a knowing hand.

"You were saying?" she teases.

Oh fuck. This is worse. I may not be touching her, but her hand on me... The blood floods my dick, leaving my mouth speechless and my brain completely empty.

"I'm, um... I was born..."

"That's Elizabeth?" Gracie traces the shape of my wife's hair with a fingernail.

"Yes," I breathe, feeling the familiar ache in my chest.

"She looks happy here." Gracie points to the one picture that sticks a stake in my heart every time I see it.

"Oh, she was," I say cryptically.

It's way too fucking soon to talk about Owen. My wife's ex-boyfriend. The guy she loved. The man she should have married instead of me. Yeah, I have a picture of her dancing with him at our wedding. I've compared the smile on her face as she whirled on the dance floor with him, arms wide, laughing, to the ones she took with me a billion times over the last few years.

I cannot believe I missed all the signs. They were there even on what should have been the happiest day of our lives. With me, she looked stiff. Like she was being forced to pose with a composed smile. With him? Well, the picture Gracie is studying says it all. Elizabeth was free, silly, alive. I didn't make her feel that. Another man did. Even on our wedding day.

As if picking up on the change in me, Gracie scoots a little closer, closing the gap I just tried to put between us.

"Let's close the album," she says quietly. "I feel like living in the moment."

I happily slam the album shut and move it aside. "I can get behind that. What kind of living would you like to do in this moment?"

She reaches a hand toward my chin and scratches her nails against the stubble that's growing in. "I'm thinking this is a perfect place to have a first kiss, Ryder. What do you think?"

I don't have to think. I turn on the couch and take her face in both my hands. I breathe her in as she snakes her hands up my arms, shoulders, and laces them behind my neck. I want to bury my fingers into her hair and get lost in the soft, warm layers. Caress her neck, her ears, her chin with my lips, exploring every sensitive inch of skin.

But she's the one who kisses me first. Her lips are so soft, so gentle as they press against mine. She seems as eager to taste me as I am to explore her. She holds my chin in her hand and nuzzles my stubble with her nose. Then I feel the slightest flick as she teases my lower lip with her tongue.

I'm twisting toward her, feeling as awkward as a kid on a first date trying to hold her, feel her, get as close to her as I can while we're side by side on the couch.

I let her take the lead as long as I can, allowing her to set the pace. She devours my skin with small, hot kisses. My cheeks, my chin, my neck. When she finally presses her lips to mine, I can hardly slow my body's response. I claim her lips with mine, giving in to the surge of electricity that draws my buzzing limbs to her.

She makes tiny purring noises with every gasp of breath. She is as colorful and sweet and delicious and erotic as I imagined. When I open my eyes, I see the wings of her eyeliner, her perfect brows, the inky blue images on her tattooed fingers as they hold my face.

I slam my eyes shut and give over to the moment. No more thinking. No more looking. All I want to do is feel her. Feel the heat of her mouth when I open mine and taste her. She does not disappoint. Our tongues tangle in a nearly frantic bid for control.

I'm breathless and hard as a goddamn baseball bat when she shoves me back against the couch and climbs into my lap, then pulls my face close. If this were a movie, this would be about the time when Luke would come down the stairs or Cora would start crying on the monitor. But my kids are sound asleep, and Gracie is moving my hand from her hip to her breast.

I moan through our kiss, and her breath hitches. I'm sure she feels the raging erection between us, and I realize there's just no good way for this to end. I can't take her upstairs. I won't. I haven't done that with anyone since Elizabeth died. I'm a father. And as much as I feel like tearing the tank from her shoulders and tasting every inch of her skin, that kind of thing just can't happen spontaneously.

I'm sure she senses my hesitation. She eases her mouth from mine and pulls back, looking into my eyes. She's even more gorgeous now. Her face is flushed, and her lips parted. The perfect, silky hair is mussed from my hands weaving through it. Her lids are half closed, but even through the erotic haze that consumes both of us, I can tell she's looking at me with concern.

"Hey," she says. "Too much? Everything okay?"

"Too okay," I grumble. I look down at my lap and slide my hands out from under her hair. "You are fucking amazing, Gracie. I just want to be able to enjoy you without worrying a kid's going to come down the stairs."

"You're right. We're responsible adults. We can control our…urges, right?"

"Totally. Urge control. Got it." Even as I say the words, I'm pulling her in. Tasting her again because now I know she's going to leave. I practically asked her to, but I want her to know it's not what I want to do. It's what I need to do. "Nope," I whisper. "You undo me. I'm powerless. You're everything I want, Gracie, and fuck. You're right here for the taking. I want you."

She's trembling as our kisses soften and ease from hungry and hard to gentle.

"I want you too," she whispers.

But wanting and having are two different things.

Reluctantly, we disengage, Gracie pulling herself from my lap and standing to smooth her clothes.

"Well," she says brightly, tugging her top back into place. "This was fun. We'll have to do it again as soon as possible."

"Yeah?" I ask. "You want that?"

Instead of answering, she pulls me close for a sweet, soft kiss.

"Yeah, I want that." She reaches out a hand and tugs me to standing, then nestles against my chest and hugs me. "But if I keep kissing you tonight, I can't be responsible for what happens. And I know tonight isn't the night for anything more. So, I'm going to say goodnight. Until next time."

I hold her firmly against me, breathing in her hair. I try to memorize the scent of her so I can hold it even when she's not with me. When I finally let her go, she looks into my face, and we grin like idiots. Like teenagers. This was fun. This was good. No drama. No games. Gracie is the real deal. More real than anything I've known.

She turns away but laces her fingers through mine. She leads me to the door, where she slips on her sandals and grabs her purse.

"Leave that key under the mat, Ryder." She gives me a grin full of promise, then I watch as she walks to her car. She starts it up, waves goodbye, and drives off into the night.

It's by far the best first date I've ever had. And it feels like the start of forever.

CHAPTER 9
GRACIE

"BABE, you posted for the shop last night? I could fucking kiss you."

Romy drops a small white paper bag on my station. "I noticed it had been a few days." She winks at me before scurrying to her station.

"If what I think is in that bag is in that bag, I'm going to kiss your face," I say, unwrapping a peanut butter crisp. I don't know how the hell she snagged one, but it smells fresh so I'm not going to ask.

"She's a suck-up," Toni, another amazing artist at my shop, says before she sticks a finger in her mouth like she's going to gag herself.

"You could learn a thing or two from her," I say, pulling the cookie from the bag and pretending to eat it right in front of her. We're actually not allowed to eat at our stations, but Toni gets the point.

She blows me a kiss because even though we diss each other constantly, we love each other to bits. Staff comes and goes in this business, but Toni has been here since the beginning. We have each other's backs when it comes to just about any drama that comes up in the shop.

Toni sees everything in life as a fight. She tends to see the negative, and I get that's just how some people are wired. But she won't offer anything, ever. Not to take out the trash, not to cover the phones. One of her favorite lines is "Not part of my job description," and while I can't help but agree with her at times, that attitude is the only thing that ever really causes us to clash.

If she cares about the cookie Romy brought me, she doesn't really linger on it. Toni asks about my schedule for the day, and we bitch for a few minutes about how the last weeks of summer have passed way too fast and all we've been able to do was play catch-up.

Since The Body Shop reopened, every day has been absolutely chaotic. While our shop was closed for cleaning, our clients were anxious to get back on our schedule to get their tattoos done. Every chair has been full, and most days, Echo is so busy answering phones that the rest of us have to chip in and do things that normally aren't our jobs, which has made Toni frazzled and bitchy, which has me playing the mediator more than I'd like to.

And it seems as if, with every spare second I have, my thoughts can only go to one place.

Ryder.

We've been having phone dates every night since I went to his house. I've been craving more of those fucking kisses ever since I got a taste. I knew he was attractive. I mean, one look at his sculpted thighs and shoulders...and then those chocolate-brown eyes that would melt any woman who isn't made of stone. I'm sure we look like total opposites together, but somehow, the way he felt under my lap, the touch of his hands in my hair... God, the taste of him. We fit like we are made for each other.

Since our make-out session at his place, things have definitely progressed. We haven't even gone on a first date yet—not a real one at least—but our attraction is off the freakin' charts.

But I'm brought back to reality when my phone buzzes, and I check the caller ID.

My gut turns over when I see who it is. My doctor's office. I debate actually answering it. Running outside so I can have a few minutes of privacy and deal with whatever this is. But the stronger part of me, the part that wants no distractions before I start inking someone's body, wins.

I let it go to voice mail. I'm not dealing with it. Not today. I've got clients back-to-back, a backlog of designs to catch up on. Email and voice mail and... Yeah, I know. They're all excuses. The trivia and bullshit of everyday life that I'm putting ahead of my health. I know that's exactly what I'm doing.

I shut off the ringer, grab my purse and phone, and go into the bathroom. I close the door and splash water on my face. My heart is racing, and I feel overwhelming guilt and fear.

This is so stupid. I scold myself.

It's my doctor, not a bill collector.

My doctor wants what's best for me, and it's not like they are in the business of stalking patients. But no matter how I try to console myself, I lean my hands on the cool porcelain, fighting tears.

Whatever it is, it's already there, I remind myself.

But the reassuring words do nothing to calm the flutters in my stomach. The tears that have been threatening to spill out finally do. I don't fight it. I just sit on the toilet and let them flow. If I'd fought them, I'd end up feeling even worse and just making myself sick. And I need to be clearheaded and calm to work.

I let myself fall apart for a few minutes, yelling internally at myself.

Why am I so afraid of not being able to have kids? I'm thirty-one. I have a great life, a great job. It's not like my life couldn't be complete without them. I could adopt… I could… end up with a man who already has kids.

That kind of thinking is dangerous, and I know it. I've only known Ryder for a couple of weeks.

I spin the roll of toilet paper and wad some two-ply up in my hands. Blot my eyes, blow my nose, then flush.

"Yo, Gracie, you almost done in there? I got to shit." Toni's voice carries through the closed door.

"Are you serious right now?" I bark. "I'm in here. Go crap in the other bathroom."

I'm half certain Toni's being nosy. It's probably because she cares. But still, I'm pissed that whatever I need to do in the bathroom is interrupted. It's nobody's business, and we have two stalls for a reason.

"Don't you have a client?" she calls through the door. "Sis, you got to come out eventually."

I wait until I hear her walking away to blow my nose again and wash my hands. Then I look in the mirror, and it's obvious I'm not going to be able to hide that I was crying. Toni caught me looking just like this in this exact same place a dozen times after everything that happened with Levi last year.

Same year, different problem.

Or maybe it's the same problem. Me not facing up to what really needs to be done. Me jumping in too fast with a guy and getting my heart obliterated in the inevitable fall.

I grab some makeup and decide I have to load it up. My face will be puffy and red for at least an hour, and the last thing a client wants to see is an emo artist. I reline my eyes and add some mascara, then blink fast as the tears threaten to undo everything I just touched up.

Why the fuck am I so emotional about something, when I don't even know what's at stake?

I paint on a perfect dark red lip, dab a little concealer under my eyes, wash my hands again, and shake out my hair.

I've got this. I've fucking got this.

No matter what it is, I have been through the hardest parts already. I'm sure of it. Or maybe that's what I'm afraid of. That what I've been through already nearly broke me. And maybe what's ahead is going to feel even worse.

But today is not a day to doomscroll through my memories. I have work to do. A job I love. And reasons to walk through the shop with a smile on my face. Even if it takes a mountain of makeup to cover up my tears.

When I finally leave the bathroom, Toni is at her station, talking to a customer who's already in the chair. She throws me a look, but I ignore her and head straight for Echo, who's waving at me through the peekaboo window in the door. I head toward her and yank open the door to see her shifting from one high-gloss Doc Marten boot to the other.

"What's up?" I ask, hoping I don't look as bad as I suddenly feel.

Echo shrugs. She digs through a purse that looks like a brown grocery sack behind the counter and then points to three familiar faces standing on the sidewalk outside. "Somebody's here to see you." She frowns. "Says he doesn't have an appointment."

"I'll be right back," I say to Echo and then push through the glass door.

Ryder is standing on the sidewalk. Luke is holding Cora's hand, while Ryder holds two cups of coffee, one in each hand. Pinched between two fingers is a small white paper bag.

"Good morning," he says. "You look beautiful."

"Dad, it's not morning," Luke scolds.

"You're right about that, buddy." He's talking to Luke, but his eyes… God, his eyes. Ryder looks at me like he wants to devour me. He licks his lips, and a grin so seductive crosses his face every inch of my body tingles. The memory of what I did to myself while thinking of him last night rushes back to me, and I know I'm blushing hard.

"Good morning and good afternoon," I say, dragging my eyes from Ryder and bending down to greet the kids. "What are you all up to today?"

"Last Friday of summer vacation," Ryder says. "Monday, Luke starts first grade."

"Wow." I give Luke a smile. "Are you excited? All my brothers and I went to Star Falls Elementary. Do you know who your teacher is yet?"

Luke nods. "Mrs. Lee."

"No way." I clap my hands. "Mrs. Lee is the best. She must be about a hundred years old now. Both Benny and I had Mrs. Lee for first grade. You're going to love her."

Ryder's watching my every move with a look so dirty, I feel like even the kids are going to pick up on the heat between us.

I turn my attention to Cora. "And what about you, sweetie? What are you going to do while Luke is in school?"

I already know the answer to this because Ryder and I have been talking about it all week, but I want to hear if she's excited. I can tell by the pout on her little face that she's not.

"I have to go to the new babysitter," Cora says, grimacing.

"Well," I say lightly, flicking a glance up at Ryder, "I hope she's fantastic. I'm sure you're going to have so much fun."

"We brought you something." Ryder holds out a coffee cup and the paper bag.

"If this is what I think it is," I say, trying not to think about the cookie I already have at my station. This is definitely a two peanut butter crisp day. "I'm going to have to find a way to thank you."

"That's what I'm hoping for," Ryder teases. "I can admit when I have ulterior motives."

"Dad, what's an—"

"I'll explain it to you later, buddy," Ryder says, cutting Luke off.

I smirk at him, take the bag and the coffee, and lean close enough that I can murmur, "I can't wait to show my appreciation."

He chuckles, a low rumble in his chest. "I had another reason for wanting to visit you today," he says.

I raise a brow at that and grin. "Hmm? There's more?" I'd tease him and maybe even risk a discreet kiss on the cheek just so I could smell him, but a really attractive young guy, probably in his mid-twenties, walks up to the sidewalk, pointing at me.

He looks from me to Ryder. "Hey. Are you Gracie? I recognize you from the website."

I take a step back from Ryder and squint into the sun.

I nod at the guy.

"I'm a couple minutes early. I thought maybe we could go over a few last-minute changes to the design."

"Sure thing," I tell him. I motion toward the door. "Check in with Echo at the counter. I'll be right in."

I turn back to Ryder, whose sexy grin is gone. "That's your tattoo client?" he asks.

I laugh at his ridiculousness.

"Try not to fall for any of your clients until I get a chance to woo you," Ryder says. I listen for any real note of jealousy, but I don't detect any, which brings a grin back to my lips.

"Woo me?" I shake my head. "You're lucky I only fall for almost-clients. Not ones I actually work on," I say, meeting his eyes.

Well, at least that's the rule now since the last client I worked on and then slept with ended in absolute disaster.

He sucks in a breath and smiles, his teeth so pretty that I wish I could feel them against my skin.

I look back at the shop. "I'd better get to work."

"Have a great day, Gracie," he says.

We stand there on the sidewalk, and I don't know what we should do, but it's clear we're both debating something. A hug? A kiss?

But then Ryder looks down at his kids and gives me a look that promises *soon*.

I sigh, knowing this is how it has to be.

CHAPTER 10
RYDER

NOW THAT WE'RE three weeks into the school year, the entire Cooper clan seems to be settling into a routine. Luke loves first grade. His teacher, Mrs. Lee, has more than lived up to the hype. She is patient and sweet, and when Luke is too overwhelmed to say much, she spends extra time making sure he participates.

I've been swapping emails with her and am pleased to learn he's now raising his hand and seems to have no hesitation to speak when called on. He even has a little group of friends he plays with every day on the playground. I'm just relieved he seems happy. Well-adjusted. I'm not sure I can say the same for me.

Cora, on the other hand, is clearly not loving her daycare situation. I've considered bailing half a dozen times on the woman who offered to help. She's great, but Cora has just been… I don't know.

Maybe it's a toddler thing or a separation anxiety issue that's new since I've never left her with anyone.

Every morning when I drop Luke off at school, we wave goodbye to her brother. I turn on some happy kid music and hope we can avoid the waterworks, but by the time I'm turning up the block toward the babysitter's house, the tears start.

She doesn't usually throw big tantrums, but when she does, it kills me. The fat tears, the trembling lip. Every day I have to leave her to go to work, I question all my choices.

Did I make a mistake not getting babysitters for my kids earlier? When they were young enough to adapt easily to new people.

Am I wrong to be back at work now?

Maybe it is too soon.

And to be honest, teaching isn't the thrill it always has been for me. Yeah, it's only a couple weeks into the year and everything is new for me too, but that's never been an issue. I meet people easily. I get along with everybody. Sports form immediate bonds, so whether I'm coaching or teaching, I find my place and fill my role, and the pieces just fall into place effortlessly.

At least, they used to.

It's nothing specific about Star Falls High. Nice people, engaged educators. The usual teacher drama. An assistant principal who seems to hate kids but expects them to find his weird, trying-too-hard sense of humor funny. You know, the typical stuff.

As much as Star Falls is starting to feel like home, teaching doesn't feel like the fit it once did. And that scares me.

Financially, I could take another year off work. But I feel like I've spent the last three years delaying the inevitable.

But I don't know if what I'm going through is normal transition anxiety or a real sign that I'm not the same man I was before.

Obviously, Elizabeth is gone. The transition back to something that feels normal was always going to hurt. I just wish I felt more confident that I'm doing it the right way. That the life I'm building is the life I still want. I never imagined I'd be doing all of this alone.

Except, I don't feel completely alone.

Whatever this is with Gracie, it's growing day by day. She's the first woman I've ever spent this much time just getting to know. It's been two months since I soaked my sneakers at The Body Shop, and we haven't shared more than a few angsty, rushed kisses.

If I never solve my childcare situation, we'll pass into the "old married couple" phase of sexless companionship before we ever get to the good stuff.

As I pull into the teachers' lot at the high school, it's between bells. Thousands of kids are switching classes, and a few who know me call out greetings as we pass in the hall.

"Hey, Coach Cooper." A group of freshmen boys tumbles over one another roughly.

"Hey, we're walking in the halls, right, guys? We're walking." I can't help but remind them that they can be friendly with me, but I'm still here to keep order and enforce the rules.

"Morning, Coach Coop." The nickname is followed by a chorus of giggles that I am sure comes from some of the sophomore girls whose class I subbed in last week.

I give them a neutral nod and a stern, "Good morning. Have a great day." I learned my first year of teaching that, as a young guy who some might call good-looking, making sure I don't encourage crushes or inappropriate attachments in my students starts with setting an example.

Friendly but not too friendly.

Firm but not mean.

Boundaries are everything, and that rule has kept my work life clean and my personal life clear.

Well, at least as far as my own behavior is concerned.

I hit the teacher's lounge and review my schedule for the day. For as long as I'm only part time, I'm on permanent sub duty, filling in where needed.

That means during the hours I'm on the clock, I can be dragged into any class where a teacher needs a sub. When there are no classes to sub, I pitch in and help the PE staff, which mostly means I help move and sort equipment and spend a lot of time in the athletic gym talking with the coaches.

The plan is for me to start coaching full time next fall and teach my own classes, but I'm starting to have my doubts about whether I can do it.

Before I was a single dad, my school and my athletes were my everything. I got up early, my head swimming with ideas and inspiration. Conditioning plans and drills excited me. I watched hours of game footage and practice tapes and rehearsed the pep talks I'd give the kids before games.

Now, I'm a full-time coach in a job that never ends. It's not that I don't still love sports, but whenever I think about throwing my whole heart and soul into anything new, I feel exhausted. Drained. It's not just doing this without a partner, although that's definitely part of it.

Moving to Star Falls was supposed to jump-start my return to reality, but I realize now that the change of scenery has only made me question myself and everything I've chosen even more deeply.

As I'm reviewing the instructions left for me by the teacher who's out sick, I feel a buzz from my phone.

Finally coming up for some air. I have tomorrow completely off. No clients, no sketching. I can literally unplug and maybe drag my favorite high school teacher away for a lunch break. Is that a thing? Can you get away for a few minutes tomorrow?

Gracie's first real day off since The Body Shop flooded and she wants to spend it with me.

Heat travels through my belly as I think about what we could do with a few unsupervised hours during the day. Before I reply, I check my schedule for tomorrow. I'm scheduled to teach PE and to cover a study hall for a teacher with a planned absence.

Fuck.

After dropping Cora off at day care, I make it to

school by nine. Even with a part-time schedule, I have to work enough hours per week to be eligible for union benefits and everything else. I just can't leave campus for a lunch break that easily.

I hate to have to tell her no. I don't want to tell her no. But, yet again, fate doesn't seem to want to make anything easy.

That night, after I put the kids to bed, I text Gracie to see if she's up for a video chat. She replies right away.

Just home from work and about to shower. Can you give me fifteen mins? I'll be quick. I don't want to keep you up too late, Coach.

She follows up the message with a little shower emoji and a winky face. I send her back a thumbs-up and then settle back into bed with a bottle of water as I scroll through some job listings, feeling a little lost and a lot frustrated.

If I leave teaching, I have no clue what else I would do. I must lose track of time because before I realize how long I've been scrolling, Gracie calls.

I pick up on the first ring.

"Hey," I say, letting the first real smile take over my face.

She immediately looks serious. "You okay? You look tired or mad. Tell me what this is I'm seeing." She motions at the screen.

"Yeah," I chuckle. "Annoying thoughts in my head.

I'm a lot better now, though. How are you? I'm really sorry I can't meet you tomorrow."

She lifts a brow at me and gives me that skeptical look I love so much. "You're deflecting," she accuses. "No deflecting. What's going on?"

I sigh. "I feel like I've lost interest in teaching," I admit. "It's all I've been trained to do, but somehow, it's different now. It's not like before."

"Before," she says gently. "Before you lost your wife?"

I don't want her to think this is all about Elizabeth because, really, it's not. "Sort of," I explain. "Before we had kids, mostly. Now, the idea of spending all day every day taking care of someone else's kids…even as a job…" I rub my face and groan. "I don't know. I'm not making any sense. I'm rambling."

"You do make sense," she says. She adjusts her camera view, and I can see she's wearing a T-shirt with the sleeves cut off and the collar cut to be much wider. The thin fabric slips off her shoulders and past her collarbone. She must see where my eyes are because she points a finger at me. "Hey, eyes up here, sexy."

"Busted," I say. "Sorry. But in my defense, have you seen yourself?"

She grins and rolls her shoulders back, so her cleavage is even more pronounced.

"You don't play fair."

"How about this?" she says. "You talk for three whole minutes about what's going on, no deflecting, no excuses, and I'll reward you."

A wicked grin claims my lips. "What's my reward?" My dick is already semi-hard just imagining what she wants to share.

"It depends on how you do." She lifts her brows and nods at me. "So, talk. Timer starts now."

I sigh but agree. If I ever want to face what I'm really feeling, I've got to admit it to myself.

"When Elizabeth passed, she left behind some money," I explain. "Not a lot. She had some life insurance from her job, and her parents had taken out a policy when she was a kid. We had some savings too, which I lived off until I sold our condo and moved here."

"Why did you leave Columbus?" she asks, adjusting herself into a more comfortable position on her bed. "I mean, wouldn't it have been easier to stay close to your friends and your in-laws?"

I cover my mouth and yawn. "Sorry," I say, "not the company." I debate how much to tell her. I've never explained what happened with Elizabeth. Is there ever really a good time? "I, uh, got into a little trouble after Elizabeth passed."

She quirks up one of those brows, and I smile even though what I'm about to share is far from funny. "So, you're a felon?" she teases. "All that identity theft talk wasn't just jokes?"

I shake my head. "Nothing that white-collar," I admit. "The story is long, but I'll make it short. Elizabeth got pregnant with Luke while she was on a break from her forever on-again, off-again boyfriend. I didn't know it at the time, but I was the rebound guy. And I knocked her up. We'd been dating about eight months, and she said she really wanted to try to make things work with me."

I'm not able to hold back my sadness. It still makes me feel like shit, even now. "Elizabeth thought I was the whole package, you know? A teacher, stable job. A better father figure than the other guy, Owen, would have been." I laugh, a bitter, grating sound. "I didn't realize when we got married that she was still completely hung up on Owen. She wanted the dream, but she wanted it with the guy she loved, and that man was not me."

Gracie moves the phone closer to her face. She looks tearful, and her lips are parted. "Ryder, I'm so sorry. I can't imagine you being anyone's second choice."

When she says that, real anger flushes my cheeks. "Thank you. That means a lot."

I wave a hand in front of my face, trying to force the feelings to keep moving. I have a little more to get out, and I'd rather do it and not fall to pieces sharing it.

"Spoiler alert. Having Luke didn't save our marriage." I shake my head and can't resist a sad smile. "We were in the process of separating when Elizabeth got pregnant again. That's right…Oops number two."

Gracie's lips are pressed firmly together like she's biting back tears, so I try to lighten the mood.

"Potent swimmers," I say. "I should maybe double or even triple bag in the future."

Maybe my joke is in poor taste because Gracie pales and doesn't look at all like she thinks it's funny.

"I'm sorry," I tell her. "This is a shitty thing to joke about." I groan. "I'm a mess, Gracie. My life is a mess. I wouldn't blame you if you cut and run now. I really hope you don't," I say, meaning every single word, "but now's probably the time. I'm getting…attached to you."

She's quiet for a moment and just looks at me through the video feed. "I'm waiting for the felony part? So, did you get carted off to jail for stealing boxes of condoms because you couldn't afford to double-bag it?"

I chuckle. "Right. That's where the story gets good. Both of Elizabeth's pregnancies were smooth, and of course, once we found out she was expecting again, we hit pause on getting separated. But as soon as Cora was born, Elizabeth developed a heart condition that I guess is very rare. She was sleeping while the kids were napping and went into heart failure. Didn't know the signs, and she passed. Here's where it gets even uglier."

I sniff hard and brace myself for what I have to share. "It turns out that her ex-boyfriend had a key to our place. He was supposed to come to the condo to see her that day, and when she didn't answer his calls or come to the door, he let himself in. My wife's former lover is the one who found her dead in our bed."

Gracie must drop her phone because I see a flurry of movement, and then the camera is facing the ceiling. "For fuck's sake. No fucking way." I hear her shouting, and then a wild swath of color covers the camera before she's holding the phone upright again. "Ryder," she breathes. "I don't even know what to say."

I nod. "It's okay. It's a lot, I know. So anyway, Owen called the ambulance but did not bother calling me. The hospital called me when they pronounced her dead."

The story gets a little ridiculous from there.

The fucking mess of calling Elizabeth's parents.

"When I laid eyes on Owen at the hospital, I tried to tackle him. I planned on beating his face in, but I ended up twisting my knee, falling to the floor, and going to the hospital myself for an X-ray. Didn't even land a punch."

She's quiet now. I can almost see her mind working a million miles a minute.

"Gracie," I grit out. "It's okay if this is a lot. It's been a lot for me. My life has been full of disappointments and missteps. I left Columbus for a fresh start, but yeah. This is all a fucking lot. I know." I wish I could tip her chin, look into her eyes, and reassure her with a touch. Hold her close.

Instead, I bring the phone farther from my face so she can't see the tightness of my smile as I fight an unexpected wave of emotion.

"I don't feel like it's a lot," she says quietly. "It's life. If your shit's heavy, well, mine is too. I get it. Thank you for sharing all of this. I just wish I could hold you. Hug you. Let you know that none of this changes what I think about you. Except the Owen part. I really hope you beat his ass eventually."

I chuckle and shake my head. "By the time reality

set in, I was too worried about raising a newborn and a toddler on my own to deal with assault charges. Besides, if I really did beat the asshole to a pulp, I could have lost my teaching license. Back then I just...I was just reacting. I felt so deceived. Like my whole life had been a lie. And then there were these two kids... They were the only things that kept me tethered to reality. I don't know what I would have done without them. Everything was a mess and I wanted to blame Owen, but in the end...it wouldn't have changed anything."

Gracie sits upright and holds the phone a little closer to her face. I can see a gravity in her eyes that melts me. "Ryder, I really want to see you. A conversation this heavy shouldn't happen over the phone."

"You want this?" I ask, not sure I can believe what I'm hearing. "After everything I've shared, you're not running for the hills?"

"If you'd let me," she says, her voice thick, "I'd come to your place. Right now. Tonight."

"I want that," I tell her. "I don't care if it's late or if it's strange. I want to see you."

She gets out of bed and steadies the phone on something with the camera facing her. "You're not streaming this over the internet, are you?" she teases.

"Of course I am," I say. "I want the entire universe to know about my sordid past."

While I watch, she wiggles out of her sleep shorts and gifts me a nice view of her bare ass. My dick takes notice, and I clench my fists, groaning at the sight. She's even more gorgeous and far more toned than I've seen under those shredded jeans.

She pulls on a pair of comfy-looking sweatpants and drags a cardigan over her sleep shirt. Then she looks into the camera. "Are we doing this?" she asks and I nod. "See you in fifteen minutes?"

I lean forward and stare into her stunning gray eyes. "The key is under the mat."

CHAPTER 11
GRACIE

WHEN I GET to Ryder's, he's standing in the open front door. I'm wearing a pair of trashy sweats and a cardigan over my T-shirt without even a bra to keep the girls from bouncing, but I don't care. I practically run up the driveway and launch myself into his arms.

We don't speak.

He just holds me, fists the back of my hair, and presses my head to his heart. I can feel its steady beat through the soft fabric.

I hold him as tightly as I've wanted to for the last two months. Through every flirty text, every video chat, every longing look we traded over a table, a child, or a coffee… It all comes together in this moment.

The front door is still wide open when he lowers his face to mine. He claims my lips with his in a first tentative kiss. Just a taste. A touch that sends my body into overdrive and my heart into outer space. I reach my fingers to the back of his neck and gently scratch my way through his hair. Our mouths open, and we deepen the kiss, his tongue dipping past my lips to explore me.

He tastes fucking divine. Better than I'd remembered and more addictive than a peanut butter crisp. Our mouths fit together perfectly, and we kiss and taste and grope until finally he pulls back, gasping for air.

"Come in. Please." His words are as ragged as his breathing. I follow him inside, and he locks the door, then looks a little shy. "Upstairs? Downstairs? I don't know what comes next."

I take his hand and lead him to the couch. There is a large afghan and enough throw pillows to make this the perfect place to do what I came here to do. Hold him. Be with him.

I have no intention of fucking him, and I practically say it out loud, so my body is forced to pay attention. I want him. That kiss was more than enough to show me that our first kiss wasn't a fluke. We have the heat. But it's way too soon to dance with this kind of fire.

He's got some potent swimmers, and I have unresolved fertility issues. There's no reason to make things harder than they have to be. Sex is off the table, but that's not what I came here for anyway. Despite how tempting he looks in his thin, form-fitting sleep sweats and ultra-soft tee. Despite how my body feels like it's finally waking up after a long, uncomfortable sleep.

I don't say a word as I settle into the cushions and strip off my cardigan. I toss it over the back of the couch and pat my chest. "Here." I murmur just the one word and he complies.

He climbs onto the couch and angles his legs so they intertwine with mine. He curls onto his side and rests his face between my throat and collarbone. We lace fingers and tighten our hands together.

"So, all I had to do was spill my trauma in your lap to get you alone?" He whispers the words against my thin top, and I untangle my fingers from his and stroke his hair.

I don't want to speak. We've done nothing but talk for months now. The flirting and the banter have been great, but if you want to really know someone, you need to spend time in their space.

Sharing the quiet.

Sharing peace.

I run my fingers through his hair and scratch lightly against his head.

"This is torture," he whispers. "Having you here like this. But the best kind. Don't stop, okay? Can you stay with me, Gracie?"

I feel his hard cock pressing against my thigh, but I say nothing and only nod.

I hear the white noise machine that must be running in Cora's room. I close my eyes and inhale the rich scent of Ryder's hair, the clean shampoo and soap smell of him refreshing and real. This is a place that feels good. It feels like home. I can't imagine a man like this ghosting me. I can't imagine anything beyond resting my head against the pillows and staying here until the sun comes up.

After just a few minutes, I feel his body relax and his breathing grows even. I close my eyes and let my head fall back against the throw pillows. I'm more comfortable than I think I've ever felt in my life.

I feel safe.

Accepted.

Wanted.

Loved.

And I let those feelings wash over me while I cover our legs with the afghan, until I, too, fall fast asleep.

The incessant buzzing of my phone in my purse wakes me. I try to open my eyes, but they are sealed shut. I grumble and then realize I can't move.

Ryder is fast asleep, not in the same position he was when we crashed, but he's still beside me, our bodies curled together like nestled spoons.

I can tell by the faint light seeping in through the windows that it's early. And if someone is calling or texting me at this hour, it's serious.

I reluctantly slip from Ryder's arms and untangle myself from the blankets before scrambling toward the front door where I left my purse.

With one eye half closed, I fumble for my phone and check the messages. There are six in all, each in escalating urgency. I read them from oldest to newest.

Gracie, honey, I came up to say goodnight and saw you weren't in bed and your car was gone. Text me when you're home so I know you're safe.

Gracie, honey, it's well after midnight. I'm not sure if you're out or if I should call the police. Your father's convinced me to wait until morning, but please, baby, call me when you see this.

Gracie, this is your mother. Are you safe? Honey, please… Call me when you get this. Lucia.

I don't bother reading the last two from this morning. I pick up the phone and dial home. Ma answers on the first ring.

"Oh my God, sweetheart."

"Ma." I cut her off, talking softly. "I'm so sorry. I came over to Ryder's and fell asleep on the couch. I should have left you a text or something. I didn't expect to stay the whole night."

"Honey," Ma says, "I have been sick with worry. Do you know how much I love you? You've been so quiet and so off since last year. I didn't know what to think, what to do." She pauses and sucks in a breath. "Will you be home later today?"

"Yeah. I'll be home in a bit."

"I did call the police and tried to make a report. They told me you were an adult and I'd have to wait a ridiculous number of days before I could file a missing persons report."

"Ma, for real? You did not."

"I did. I'm sorry. You've been so distant, and you've been so stressed with the stuff going on at the shop…"

"Ma, I'm so sorry," I say seriously. "Can you get some rest? I'm off work today. Maybe we can spend the day together. After you take a good nap."

She's sniffling, and I hear a lot of racket, which probably means she's trying to hold the phone to her ear while she fumbles around for tissues.

"Yeah, honey, of course. I'm supposed to help Bev at the shelter today, and then Carol and I were going to meet Sassy for lunch. It's her day off from Benito's, and…"

"Okay, Ma, we'll talk when I get home."

"I love you, Gracie," Ma says.

"I love you," I say on a whisper.

When I end the call, Ryder is standing in the doorway of the kitchen, looking concerned. "Everything all right?"

"I'm a fucking idiot. I didn't tell my parents I was leaving last night. My mom went in to say goodnight and apparently spent the whole night thinking I'd run away from home or been kidnapped."

Ryder's smile is small and stiff. "You're a little old to be kidnapped, but I get it." He looks at me with worry in his face. "Why would she think you ran away from home?"

Now that he's opened up to me, I should tell him everything. But I'm not ready to. Not yet.

I have some unfinished business that I need to handle first. And I want to handle it on my own. The last thing I want is my mother or a boyfriend or anyone coming in to save the day. I don't want to be like

Ryder's ex. I still can't believe that woman hid so much from the man she was supposed to share everything with.

And then there's Levi, the hotshot athlete whose star shines so bright, he thinks he is untouchable.

I'm a woman with flaws and faults. But before I share everything with Ryder, I want to bring him a story that may not have a happy ending, but a story where I'm my own hero.

I lift my face from his chest and loop my arms around his waist. I meet his eyes. "I haven't exactly been honest with my mom about things going on in my life lately." That's true; it's just not the entire truth. "There's more I want to share with you when we have time to talk, but I should get home and clear the air with her." I take him by the hand and lead him back to the couch. We sit side by side and hold hands in silence. "You know," I say quietly, "I'd like to date you, Ryder. Get to really know you. See if there is as much between us as I think there might be."

He tightens his grip on my fingers. "Hell yes. I'm in. If you're not already scared away, you're…" He grows quiet, and I bite back a smile.

Slow and steady. That's how this relationship has been. No flare, no wildfire. But the strongest things are forged over time, so maybe…just maybe.

"Would you consider letting my parents babysit Luke and Cora so we can go on a real date?" I throw out the suggestion that I've been sitting on for a while now.

It means bringing Ryder into the Bianchi universe, but after this morning, that cat is out of the bag for good. I don't want him to feel pressured, though. "You can bring them to my parents' house if you'd be comfortable with them there. Or I can ask my mom if she'll come here. This isn't just me trying to get you alone. I mean, it is. But the kids' safety comes first. Ahead of my dirtier needs."

Ryder's massive smile dims just a bit. "I appreciate the suggestion. I do. I just don't know how the kids would feel about that," he says. "They're adjusting to a lot of new people all at once. I'd be willing to try, I just..."

I shake my head and tighten my hold on his hands. "Say no more. I get it." The tears sting my nose and eyes again. "Look at what just happened with my mom and I'm old. Your babies are your heart and your soul. I get that. I will never push something that won't be in their best interests. If you say it's a no-go, that's that."

"Thank you for understanding. You're incredible. You don't know how few women would feel the way you do."

I shrug. "Good. Less competition for all of this." I motion my hand from his head to the waistband of those wrecked sweats. "And I really want all of this."

He chuckles and loops an arm around my shoulder, pulling me close. "Why don't you invite us over to meet your parents? I know it's not the normal way these things are done, but if we meet them and the kids are okay, we'll see where it goes."

I wrap my arms around his waist and breathe him in. I close my eyes and nod against the softness of his shirt. Beneath his shirt is warm, solid muscle. That steady heartbeat.

"I like the sound of seeing where it goes."

CHAPTER 12
GRACIE

WHEN I LET myself in the front door, Ma is upstairs, and Dad is drinking coffee and reading the paper.

"Morning, sweetheart." He greets me with a kiss and not a word of warning or worry. "Coffee?"

I chuckle to myself. Leave it to Pops to act like everything is completely normal, even though I'm sure Ma kept him up all night freaking out.

I've already decided today is going to be a day of hard things. "I'd love some," I say. "Do you mind if I listen to a voice message with you? Not like with you, with you, but. Like, while we sit here?"

My dad looks at me over the stylish tortoiseshell rims of his glasses. "Not at all. Do what you got to do." He pours me a full cup of coffee and sets the mug and a spoon in front of me at the dining room table.

I punch in the voice mail code and listen to the message from my doctor.

"Hi, Grace. This is Anna from Dr. Calder's office. It's

time to book your annual exam, but there's a note in the file that the doctor wanted to schedule a hysterosalpingogram. We can't book them on the same day, but when you call back to schedule your annual, just have them pull the chart and schedule both appointments. There are some activity restrictions before the test, so you'll need to schedule based on your cycle and will need to avoid vaginal intercourse. We'll tell you more when you call to set the appointment. Thanks, Grace."

Well, that's exactly what I expected. Not better, but certainly no worse. It's time to schedule the tests. And time to face whatever the results mean.

I delete the message and take a sip of coffee.

"Everything all right, kiddo?" My pops looks at me over those glasses, and I'm overcome with love for him. I can just imagine Ryder someday sitting with Cora as she faces hard things. I believe he'll be even more involved and loving than my dad has been, which is saying a lot. My dad, even before he retired, was involved, passionate, and supportive.

It hits me then how hard it must be for Ryder to have to put his own desire for adult time, time with me, even, so far down the list of everyone else's needs.

I've only ever had to take care of myself. Pitch in with the dogs. Pick up some slack if Ma or Pops is sick. I've had such an easy life. I realize how much harder I could work. How much harder other people have it. It's a humbling realization to think through. It's gut-wrenching to look at my dad and see a glimpse into Ryder's reality.

I get up from my chair and bend over to hug my father. "Yeah, I'm okay," I say quietly. "I'm so sorry I worried you guys last night."

Just then, my mom comes down the stairs still wearing her nightgown. Her feet are in fuzzy slippers, and her auburn hair is sticking up every which way.

"Baby," she says, coming into the kitchen. "You're home."

I pull my mother into my arms, and we hug each other hard.

My dad watches the two of us, sipping his coffee and sneaking peeks at his newspaper. "Should I go?" he asks.

"No, please," I tell him. "I want to talk to both of you." I take a seat at the table and slug back some coffee. "Is now a good time?"

"I've got no place to be." My dad's grin lightens the mood. "I'm retired, kiddo. I'm permanently off the clock."

Ma nods and heads toward the kitchen to pour some coffee. "I'm not due at the shelter until ten," she says. "But I'll call out if you need me here, honey."

"No, Ma, this won't take long." I definitely don't want my mom messing up her day any more than it already is because of me. I wait until the three of us are sitting at the table with refilled coffee mugs to start talking.

"I have some things to tell you," I say, "and it's stuff I probably should have told you last year. But I haven't been dealing with any of it well."

My mom's face is drained of color, so I rush on.

"I'm fine, first of all," I say. "Nothing really bad happened, I just, well… What happened was very hard, but I'm okay. I will be."

I explain how the short fling I had with the pro football player ended suddenly. He apparently grew up nearby but went to private schools, so I never knew who he was until he came into the shop for a tattoo.

"He was here for a family wedding, I think," I explain. "We hit it off, hooked up a couple times, and then that was it. He left town." I shake my head, feeling embarrassment and shame heat my cheeks.

"He didn't say goodbye, and it's not like I thought we had any great romance or anything. We used protection," I rush on, having a hard time believing that I'm thirty-one years old and sharing the details of my sex life with my parents. But this is the truth. This is my truth, and if I am going to face what happened, that means facing all of it. "He was the only guy I'd been with in a while, and I don't know what happened. The condom broke or tore. I missed my period after he left town. I took a test, and it came back positive."

I have to pause when Ma gasps and covers her mouth. "You were pregnant, Gracie?"

I nod, tears stinging my eyes. "I was so shocked and afraid. I didn't know what to do. I called and texted, but Levi didn't reply. Not once. That felt shitty enough. I figured he didn't believe me or thought I was just some…I don't know. But then I…"

This is where I lose my words. I haven't said this out loud to anyone.

"I miscarried," I blurt out. "It was early. I texted Levi to let him know what happened." I grow bitter then, the irony and the rage and the emotions I've bottled up for so long coming out in a rush. "I didn't want him thinking I was some dumb-ass chick trying to shake him down for money. I told him I'd lost the baby and he'd never be hearing from me again."

Mom wipes her eyes, and Pops hands her the paper napkin he's been using as a coaster for his mug.

"The asshole finally responded to that text." I remember it like it was yesterday. I pull out my phone and let his words speak for themselves.

This number's not in my contacts. Who's this?

My mom's hands shake as she passes my phone to my father. He reads the words and pounds a fist on the table. "What the hell does that mean? Was he fucking around with you, Gracie?"

I shrug. "That means after I texted that I was pregnant, he probably deleted my number from his phone. He didn't block me," I explain. "Which means he could still get calls and texts from me. He was sending a message that I meant nothing to him. That what happened to me was my problem and I mean nothing to him."

"That son of a bitch." Now my father's furious. "What do we do? Do we call his agent? Call the team? What do we do?"

"Mario." Ma's voice is sharp. "Let Gracie finish.

We're not going to tweet about this and get the boy in trouble unless Gracie tells us that's what she wants."

I hold back a chuckle because I am damned sure my parents don't know what tweeting is.

"There's a little more," I say, and I firm my lips and just get on with it. "With everything that happened, my gynecologist did an ultrasound. She thinks there may be some issues going on. Nothing like cancer, so don't panic. But she wants to see if something might prevent me carrying a pregnancy to term in the future."

"Oh, sweetheart." My mom is gripping her coffee cup in two shaking hands. "What can we do? What do you need?"

I shrug. "Well, that's why I wanted to talk to you. I moved home last year because I couldn't face this alone, but I wasn't ready to deal with it at all. I haven't scheduled the tests yet. But I want to now."

"We'll drive you. We'll be in the room with you. Anything you need, Gracie. We will hold your hand through it all. Anything you need." My father's voice cracks, and his eyes shimmer with tears. "And if you can't have kids, you can't have kids. Kids aren't all they are cracked up to be."

"Mario," my mother cries out, but something about the sincerity in Dad's voice has me cracking up.

"Pops…" I laugh so hard my stomach starts to hurt. "Nice one."

My dad looks confused, like he didn't realize he made a joke, and he shrugs. "Well, I'm serious. You kids mean the world to me, but life isn't about just getting married and popping out babies."

Dad gets up from the chair and stands in front of me. "Gracie, you're an artist. You're passionate. You're the most powerful, beautiful woman. Your life has value and meaning, no matter what. Stay here forever and adopt a hundred more shelter pets. I don't care. We love you, kiddo." He squeezes my hands and looks at my mom. "The real question is who do I got to pay to crack the kneecaps of this son of a bitch?"

"Mario, stop." My mom stands up and drags her chair close to me. She cups my face in her hands. "We're not going to hurt that man. Unless you want us to."

I shake my head, knowing full well my parents are only half kidding. They'd probably wage war for me if I asked them to. And I love them for it. But Levi Olson is a selfish prick. Karma will find its way to him. My only job is to take care of myself.

"I want to forget about him and focus on me. On healing." I face my mom. "But I do have a favor to ask."

CHAPTER 13
RYDER

I'M STIRRING powdered cheese and milk into cooked macaroni noodles with one hand and flipping chicken breasts in a pan so they don't burn when my phone rings. Austin never calls, so I pick up the phone on the first ring.

"Hey, man. I'm cooking dinner. You're on speaker."

I can see Cora and Luke playing together while I cook, which warms my heart. Luke doesn't always have the patience to show his sister his trains, but since he's started school, he's learned a whole new way of dealing with other kids. Sometimes I love what I see, like now, when he's clearly demonstrating how to be patient with others. And then other times, he calls his sister a fuckface, and I have to write a carefully worded email to Mrs. Lee, asking who the hell is saying fuckface in the first grade… Yeah. The changes in my son don't always make me proud.

Parenthood, man. It's a trip.

"Ryder!" Austin sounds peppy and breathless, so basically the same as always. His consistency is one of the things I love most about him. "S'all good, brother. Hey, I'm calling for a quick favor. You got time this weekend?"

"Depends. Time for what?" I say honestly. "I kept the kids in swimming lessons, so we're busy tomorrow morning. You need me to come home? I could probably drive up after swim on Saturday."

I make sure the burner is off under the dinosaur-shaped mac and cheese and focus on not burning the chicken. My mind is already spinning. A trip to Columbus could be great. Maybe Gracie would be able to come? Ah, fuck. She works almost every Saturday, so probably not. Maybe we could go up on Sunday? She's always off on Sunday when the shop's closed.

"No, man. Nothing like that. I'm thinking about driving to you. You got a couch I can sleep on if I invite myself to Star Falls for the weekend?"

"Are you serious? Hell yeah, man. When you thinking?"

This is a surprise. Austin's always watching sports, managing games, or writing about them when he's not working his nine-to-five. For him to take a drive out to see us? I wonder what's going on to bring him out to Star Falls.

"You okay, man? Anything serious going on?"

"Serious, yeah, but not bad or anything." He sounds happy, so maybe he's met someone? News like that would hardly justify a trip out here, but he sounds even better than his usual happy self, if that's possible. "I'm not sick or anything. I just wanted to hang with you and talk. See my best friend's kids before they forget what I look like."

It's only been three months since we moved to Star Falls, but fuck, it feels like a lifetime since we left Columbus.

"Just come. You're welcome anytime. I legit mean it. This is a safe small town. I'll leave the key under the mat, and you just come whenever and let yourself in."

"Key under the mat?" Austin blows out a loud, long breath and laughs. "That is a whole world away from Columbus. But why do you need to leave a key out? You got somebody you're seeing?"

His question is a fair one, but I don't know how to answer it. "I mean, maybe? Sort of. I met someone, but…" I pierce the chicken with a cooking thermometer and watch the numbers rise. "We haven't even been on a real date yet. The childcare situation is all screwed up here. I'm interested, but so far, it's been tables for four on all our dates."

Satisfied that the chicken is done, I pull the frozen broccoli out of the freezer and let the chicken rest while I toss the whole bag into a pot of boiling water.

"Man, that sucks. Well, that settles it. I'm taking tomorrow afternoon off work. I'll be out to your place before dinner, and we can hang. Is there someplace I can take the kids Saturday night? Give you a date night while I'm in town?"

I can't believe he just offered to watch the kids. Give

me a night alone with Grace? I pick up the phone and take it off speaker. "You'd do that?" I ask.

Austin has known my kids since the moment they were born, and he's my best friend. Even though it's been three months since they've seen him, I'm sure they won't miss a beat. Even if he just stays in the house with them once I put them to bed, there's no one on earth I'd trust my kids with more than Austin.

Austin chuckles. "Fuck yeah, bro. Are you kidding? I'm coming to town to ask for some help, so I'm fully prepared to return the favor."

Help? I'm curious what Austin could possibly need help with. The guy is a perpetual motion machine and is the most driven man I know. He knows I've got my hands more than full right now, so if he's coming to see me, it's gotta be serious.

"All right," I say. "I'll see you Friday."

We end the call, and I drain the broccoli. Luke isn't gonna be happy, but I plan on introducing him to honey mustard tonight to see if that makes the greens go down a little easier.

"Luke," I call. "Take your sister and wash your hands. Dinner is ready."

Then I pick up the phone and text Grace.

I have some sort of news. If you're free this weekend, I might be able to take you on an actual date Saturday night. I still want to meet your parents, tho. Video chat later?

Since it's only five o'clock, I doubt she's free to answer, but I'm grinning ear to ear when I see a little red *100* emoji come back in response.

Luke is not at all a fan of honey mustard, but we get through dinner, toothbrushing, baths, and our bedtime ritual without any major meltdowns or disasters. By 7:55, when both kids are sound asleep and I've started a load of laundry, I text Gracie.

Call whenever you're free, gorgeous.

I add a fire heart emoji, because what the fuck. I have feelings for her. And in the last two days since she slept in my arms on my couch, all I can think about is holding her again. My body's on fire for her, and my heart is already burning with something that wants to engulf me.

She surprises me by video calling instead of replying. I lean back against my pillow and start the chat.

"Hey. That was quick. How was your day?"

"Good. Good. My last client was a no-show, which was even better," she tells me. "I caught up on some stuff that I've been putting off."

"That's gotta feel good," I say.

She nods, and I can see she's got a marker or pen stuck behind her ear.

"Were you drawing?" I point to my ear. "Marker?"

She pulls it from between the strands of her hair and laughs. "Yeah. Just fucking around. Not client stuff. Something just for me."

"Can I see sometime?" I ask. "I mean, if it's not too personal or anything."

She blinks a few times, and I feel like maybe it was personal. Maybe I touched a nerve. But she nods. "Yeah. I'd love to share it sometime."

"So…" I run a hand through my hair and pivot to the good news. "Gracie Bianchi, can I please…take you…on a date this Saturday night?"

She grins and nods. "Fuck yes. What about the kids? Do you have a sitter?"

I tell her my best buddy, who's like an uncle to the kids, is crashing with me for the weekend.

She claps her hands and rubs them together. "Holy shit. What should we do? What do you want to do? My mind is racing!" Then she grows serious. "It's Saturday, though, so I might work until like nine. I have a client at six who will definitely be there for about three hours."

I shake my head. "Doesn't matter. I'll take one hour alone with you if that's all I can get." I'm definitely disappointed that she has to work so late on the one night I can wrangle a sitter, but I look on the bright side. Austin will be here, and maybe I can convince him to wake up with the kids and feed them breakfast. If I can sleep in until even eight, I'll be able to spend a couple hours with Gracie. And that's a couple hours more than we've had in months.

She smiles. "What should I wear? What do you want to do? We could hit my brother's for a late dinner?"

I hold up a hand. "Can I plan it? Do you trust me? I have something in mind, but I want it to be a surprise."

Gracie frowns. "I fucking hate surprises." But then she softens. "But for you, yeah. I'm willing to go with it."

"I'll take willing to go with it. But note to self, no surprise parties for Grace in the future."

She laughs and shakes her head. "Will I get to meet your friend while he's here? It'll be cool to meet someone close to you instead of you always being smothered by Bianchis."

"Yeah, absolutely. Maybe we can stop by The Body Shop on Saturday between appointments. Just drop off peanut butter crisps and run."

"Are you trying to make me fall in love with you?" She lifts a brow at me, but she's grinning.

"Stop trying to ruin the surprise," I say. "I've got this master plan, and yeah, if you're madly in love with me by the end of it, then…" I shrug.

She looks straight into the camera and murmurs, "I can't believe we're going to be alone. Like real grown-ups."

"Real grown-ups, indeed," I joke. "Did you smooth things over with your mom?"

We chat a bit about that until I yawn. "Sorry," I say. "This rock-and-roll lifestyle is wearing me out."

"I still have a crick in my neck from sleeping on your couch the other night," she says. "But it was worth it."

"I think I still have a case of maddening blue balls from the other night," I tell her. "*Totally* worth it. In fact, if you want to wear that same sleep tee and no bra on Saturday…"

She lowers the phone so I get a quick view of her chest. "Already wearing that," she says. "My favorite sleepwear."

I groan. "Gracie," I say on a rough whisper. I see the

outline of her nipples through the tee. "The things I want to do to you."

"The things I want you to do to me," she purrs. "Want a sample?"

I swallow hard against the sudden dryness in my throat. Is she serious? Now? On live video?

I think of all the things that could happen and all the things that could go wrong. My Wi-Fi network is private. My kids are in bed, and a quick look at the monitor confirms that Cora is sound asleep. I'm sure by this time Luke is completely conked out, but I decide to lock my bedroom door just in case.

"I'm gonna kid-proof my room," I tell her. "Hold, please."

I jump out of bed, and the boner I'm already sporting makes it that much tougher to hustle to the door. But I manage to turn the lock with the phone still in my hand. I carefully angle the camera to show her exactly the effect her invitation has on me.

"I'd say that's a yes to the sample you're offering." I practically growl the words.

She smiles then holds up a finger for me to wait. I hear rustling and get an extreme close-up of her tee while she adjusts the camera. It looks like she's resting it against something. "Aw, fuck, hold on a sec," she says.

While she figures out how to prop up her phone, I settle back against the pillows and adjust my cock in my sweats. I wonder if I should strip them off but then think that's too much. I don't know what she has planned, so I just let my dick chafe the inside of my sweats and wait. My heart is thundering and my palms are damp with excitement when I see the lights dim in Gracie's room.

"Ambience," I say softly. "Nice."

She chuckles and then climbs back into bed. "Good view?" she asks.

"The best," I confirm. "Gracie..." I don't know what to say. It seems like we've been dating for months, and yet we've never been alone for more than a couch snuggle. She is gorgeous and sexy, and I don't know that I can pretend anymore that I don't want to go all in. That I don't want all of her. I don't care if it's hard. I don't care if it's not a "normal" way to date. Was it normal to marry a woman who wasn't over her ex? Was it normal for her to have a second kid with me, even though she'd planned on leaving? Has any of my so-called perfect life been anything close to what other people would consider normal?

"Yeah?" she prods. But I lose my words entirely while I watch her circle the fullness of her breast with her fingertips. The tip grows hard, and she tugs at a nipple through the thin fabric of her tee. "You were saying?"

"Nope. I wasn't saying a goddamn thing," I growl. I narrow my eyes and watch as she holds the weight of her ample breast between her hands. With her phone propped up, she can use both hands to touch herself.

"I'm open to suggestions," she says, flicking a glance into the camera.

"Skin." I practically beg the single word, unable to form complete thoughts. "I wanna see."

She lifts one of those perfect, dramatic, dark brows and puckers her lips like she's going to blow me a kiss. Then her hands disappear from view. One second later, the entire top lifts, and she rests the loose hem on top of her cleavage. I drink in the sight of her exposed breasts like a man dying of thirst.

"Holy fuck," I gasp. "You're even more perfect than I imagined."

"You imagined this?" she asks with a smirk.

"Only every night, morning, and probably every second shower since I met you." I can't be cool. I don't even try. I want Gracie, and the sight of her baring herself to me fills me with an urgency I can't wait to release. I want to taste the coppery peaks, suck those hard buds deep into my mouth and nibble them until she cries out my name.

She's smiling as she lowers her chin to watch herself as she twists the erect tips between her fingers.

"Do you like that?" I pant. "Tell me what makes you wet."

"You," she says. "Imagining you doing this to me."

"More," I say. "Tell me everything. Show me everything."

She cups the fullness of her breasts together and squeezes them. "Can you imagine yourself here?" she asks. She holds her tits tightly together with one hand, then licks her index finger and slides it down the line of her cleavage until it disappears.

Holy fuck. To slide myself between those tits, slippery from oil or lube or my come… I lower a hand to my cock and pant. "Fuck yes. Right there. Show me," I demand.

She nods and twists a little, giving me a perfect sideways view of her breasts. They are full, more than a handful in size, and they bounce when she opens a bedside drawer. She pulls out a black satin bag and a small bottle of lube.

She looks into the camera with heat glazing over her expression. She licks her lips and pulls open the drawstrings on the bag. "Do you want this?" she asks. "Do you want to see what I want you to do to me?"

I nod, speechless.

She pulls out a sleek black dildo that looks space-age in its design. The body of the thing isn't shaped like a realistic cock, but it has a handle, which I assume gives it a good grip for her to use on herself. I jam a hand down the front of my sweats and watch.

The cap on the bottle of lube makes a little clicking noise as she opens it and dribbles a generous amount over the shaft of the dildo.

I groan and stroke myself in time with the long, sensual strokes she uses to work the lube over the toy. When it's slippery, she leans back against her pillows and then licks just the tip of the toy with her tongue.

My eyes want to close. I want to smash my head back against the bed and jerk myself until I release, but I can't tear my eyes away from her.

She uses her left hand to cup the underside of her

breasts together, creating the perfect valley to thrust into. Holding the dildo in her right hand, she slides it between her tits, slowly moving the toy back and forth.

My hips jerk reflexively. The blood races through my limbs, and I swear to fuck, if I didn't have two kids asleep in bed right now—two kids whose safety I value above my own life—I'd be in the car on my way to her now. I'd throw her against the bed and grab the toy from her hands and take its place.

"Faster," I coax, gripping my painfully hard erection.

She does, moaning lightly as the toy slips from between her slick breasts. She thrusts faster, making her tits move as the toy disappears between the perfect flesh. She pauses and pulls the dildo out and rubs the wet tip against her nipples. Her eyes flutter closed, and I can tell by the flush that climbs across her chest that she's aroused.

I have lube of my own, but it's hidden out of kid-reaching heights in an upper cabinet in my bathroom. I normally have time to prepare to use it, but now I need it and I am not about to leave the show to get it. I do, however, keep hand lotion at the bedside as a backup. I reach for a pump of it and fill my palm.

"What are you doing out of my view?" she purrs. "Show me?"

I hesitate for only a second. I'm a teacher and a dad, and showing my cock on camera to anyone—even someone I trust as much as I trust Gracie—makes me a little nervous. She picks up on my hesitation and smiles.

"It's okay. You can just tell me. Feel like taking off your shirt so I'm not the only one topless?"

I nod. "I just squirted in my hand," I tell her. "Lotion, that is."

"Tell me more," she urges.

I stick my hand down the front of my sweats and wipe the lotion across my shaft. Then, with nearly dry hands, I pull my T-shirt over my head.

"I knew it." Her words are low and throaty. A velvet purr and an enticing sigh all at once. "You're a fucking hottie, Ryder Cooper."

I twist my lips into a half smile, but I get right back to touching myself. "You're explosive, Gracie Bianchi. I want to watch you make yourself come. Above the waist is fine, but I want to see your face."

She nods. "Yeah?" Then she takes the toy from between her breasts and bends her legs so her knees are in the view of the camera. Her tits are exposed, and I can only imagine what is happening between those legs. She operates the dildo with one arm, and I watch her tattoos move as she works the toy with one hand and lifts and teases her nipple with the other.

Her lips part, but she manages to keep her eyes open, watching me as I thrust my lotioned-up cock into my fist. I try to keep pace with her. I don't want to miss a thing, but my dick is demanding attention. I grip myself but fight the need to tug faster, harder, until her breathing turns from panting to an all-out gasp.

"*Ryder*." She grits out my name and then closes her eyes, slams her head back against the pillows, and spreads her knees even wider. She shudders silently, her tits bouncing lightly with the tremors that rock her body. I can't stop myself from coming, and with a few fast, furious jerks, I spill my whole load right into my palm.

I gasp but keep my eyes open, watching every second of her release.

I wipe my hand on my wadded-up shirt and wait until she opens her eyes to make a sound.

"I've never watched anyone titty-fuck a dildo before," I say, awe in my tone. "It might just be my new favorite foreplay."

"Just you wait," she says. "I've been pining for you for months now. I've got lots of creative ways to work out the frustration."

We talk a few more minutes and then blow each other kisses and say goodnight. By the time I end the video call, I'm happy. Satisfied. I feel complete here in Star Falls in a way I never felt back in Columbus. I'm sure of it now. I'm falling head over fucking sneakers for Gracie Bianchi.

CHAPTER 14
GRACIE

NO MATTER how many times or ways I look at the calendar, there's no changing the timing. I called my doctor the same morning I told my parents what happened.

The catch?

My test is on Tuesday. Two days *after* my first real date with Ryder.

The karmic joke's on me, because I can't have sex that close to the test.

But God do I want him. Really, really want him.

I smile as I get ready for work. This is, without a doubt, the strangest relationship I've ever been in. But it's also the most exciting. The most hilarious. Ryder can crack me up with a single emoji. And I know I've done the same for him. I'm just amazed at the way I feel. This feels real and right, even if it's far from normal.

Once I'm dressed, I head over to the small drafting table I have in my room and look over the pages. I've been putting the finishing touches on a special project I've been working on the last few weeks.

A few weeks ago, Luke and I got into a conversation about trains. He knows a lot about them, in kind of a nerdy, adorable way. Especially for a first grader. It's obvious his dad has either read him a lot of books or answered a lot of questions about trains, so I started looking for a train coloring book or kids' encyclopedia on trains, but I couldn't find anything.

I don't normally draw technical pieces. Pistons and machinery I usually leave to my colleagues, but I've been practicing drawing trains so I can maybe put together a custom coloring book or something for Christmas.

I know, I know. It's only been a few months that I've even known Ryder. Thinking about giving his kids holiday gifts is maybe a stretch. But these kinds of gifts take time. I'd rather practice making trains now and toss the whole ream of paper into the bin than wake up on Christmas morning wishing I'd spent the time when I could sneak a few minutes here and there.

Once I'm dressed and ready, I pass my brother Vito in the hallway.

"You leaving?" he asks.

"No, idiot. I just got home. I'm going to bed." I smack him before he has the chance to smack me and run down the stairs.

"Real mature, Gracie," he shouts, but he's laughing and I'm laughing.

Brothers. They never get any better, just older.

My pops is at the dining room table with his glasses in his hand, reading. I head over to kiss him goodbye, but the look on his face stops me.

"Dad?" I say. "Everything okay?"

He shrugs. "I don't know, bella. You tell me." He hands me the sports section of the newspaper.

"Just tell me," I say, anxiety starting to pool in my belly.

"That asshole," he spits, shaking his phone in the air like he wants to toss it. "That Levi Olson kid."

I taste bile in my throat and grimace. "What? What is it? Is he dead or something?"

"I only wish. He deserves no less for what he did to my daughter."

"All right, Pops. Thanks, but out with it. I need to go to work."

My pops walks over to me. He puts his hands on my shoulders and looks me square in the eye. "Something big happened. I don't know what, the news isn't saying. All I know is the team made a statement this morning that Olson's been cut. He's done. And his publicist followed the statement up with this."

My dad puts on his glasses and reads from his phone: "Levi Olson has officially terminated his position on the Cleveland Cyclones. This separation is mutual and was made with the understanding that Levi could return to play in the league and on the team at any point in the future if an agreement were to be reached. There are allegations that may be made in the media, and we urge the fans not to be distracted by unsubstantiated rumors. Levi consulted with the coaching staff, his teammates, and league officials prior to reaching this life-changing decision. His personal health and well-being come first, and he will spend the next few months away from the field to focus on himself. We'd ask that the privacy of Levi and his family be respected during this time."

I'm shocked, and it must show on my face. "What the fuck happened?" I ask.

My dad shrugs. "I've been searching every news feed I can find. I don't know what he did, but it had to be bad. The league wouldn't cut him loose mid-season unless it was a conduct violation. That or maybe drugs?"

This isn't great news for him. Whatever it is, something like that could end his career. While I should be dancing on cloud nine and popping champagne, this doesn't feel like cause to celebrate.

Someone else's downfall doesn't make me feel better about myself. I was probably just another casualty of a man whose life was already showing signs of falling apart. I wouldn't have known that, of course, until it was too late.

"Well, I'm not happy for him. Even if karma did come calling quick. Shitty situation. Thanks for telling me, though, Dad."

"Gracie," he says. "There's one more thing. There're a few stories reporting that the asshat's coming back to Star Falls. Tail between his legs kind of shit."

"What? Why the hell would he come back here?" I

knew he had family here, but…a guy with his money and connections, shouldn't he go to rehab out in Malibu or disappear abroad for a couple months?

Pops shrugs. "All I know is if I run into him, I'll take a mallet to his knees, Gracie. So help me God, I will."

I pull my pops into a hug. "Thank you," I murmur. "But, Pops. You didn't work at the steel mill for all those years to spend your retirement behind bars."

"I'm an old man. How long they going to give me?" he asks. "Ten years? I'd do ten years for you, Gracie. I'd do a lifetime if it meant getting even with the shit-stain that hurt my little girl."

I chuckle at that. "It looks like karma took care of the shit-stain for us, Dad." I kiss him on the cheek and check the time. "I got to roll. Thanks for letting me know. Does Ma know?"

He nods. "I had her run into town to set up a bail fund."

I give him a single-brow scolding, and he laughs. "Kidding. I texted her the story. She told me to tell you before you heard it on the news."

I doubt that's the kind of news that would ever reach me in my day-to-day life, but I appreciate their looking out for me. I kiss my dad goodbye and head to work, ready to put Levi Olson and the shame of my past in the grave forever.

Well, if I'd thought I could live in Star Falls even five minutes without the whole town buzzing about it, I was seriously mistaken.

The second I unlock the door to The Body Shop, Toni is coming in on my heels. "Bitch, did you hear about that hottie you inked last year?" She's wearing the most obscenely tight leopard-print leggings with a hot-pink top and an armload of jelly bracelets. She's wearing sunglasses, but the second she takes them off, she starts eyeballing me with this curious look on her face. "You know who I'm talking about, right?"

I glare at her. "No," I say.

This is exactly why I didn't tell anyone when it happened.

"We never hooked up," I lie to her, confirming the story I told everyone last year. "We had drinks, traded a few texts, and he was back to his real life."

"Maybe he wants another tattoo," she says. "If he comes back in, he fair game?"

I grimace, not entirely sure what she means. "Like, you want him as a client? Go for it. I could not care less."

I turn away from her and greet Echo, who pushes through the door looking rather plain. She's wearing a long-sleeved black shirt, a pair of black pants, and her face is free of makeup.

"What happened to you?" Toni demands, leaning on the counter while Echo punches into the app on the tablet. "You look like normal."

Echo rolls her eyes. "Job interview," she says, sounding incredibly grumpy about it.

"What?" I ask. "Why?"

Echo grabs a giant purse shaped like an old-school metal lunch box, complete with metal clasp and plastic handle. "I'm looking for something else part time. Wish me luck finding anything where I can dress the way I want."

She storms to the back, where I assume she plans to change her clothes, leaving Toni and me behind.

"She's a strange bird," Toni says.

"There's only one Echo."

"You know what I'd be doing if I were you?" Toni asks, getting back to a juicer topic and forgetting all about Echo. "I'd be reaching out to that hottie football player, and I'd try to get him out for a date. Maybe he'll spill some dirt about why he got fired. That's a story worth big money to the media. You know what I'm saying?"

"What the fuck, Toni? You want to go seduce some loser and sell his story to the press, go for it. I don't want anything to do with that shady shit."

Toni clucks her tongue and heads toward the back. "That's a mistake, babe," she says. "Look, we're not like those people. He's rich, and he's fucking over other people with his money and his position in life. Having people fuck you back just comes with the territory. I wouldn't hesitate to sell a dick pic, a story… Shit. If there was enough money in it, I don't know there's much aside from illegal shit that I wouldn't do."

There's no arguing with Toni. I'm not even going to try to change her mind. She's entitled to her views.

I'm suddenly exhausted. I check the tablet and see my client for two is confirmed. He's a regular, and he just wants a small addition to a piece I did for him two summers ago. Should take me no more than three hours, including sketching and placing the stencil.

I am relieved in some ways. Glenn is a great guy. Older man, not too chatty. Easy to talk to if I'm in the mood, but able to be quiet and let me work once I'm in the flow. It's a small gift from the universe that I'll take today because the last thing I want is to hear any more about Levi Olson.

CHAPTER 15
RYDER

I WALK into my rental house to find my buddy Austin, sleeves rolled to his elbows, feet on the coffee table, furiously typing on his laptop.

"Uncle Austin," I say as we walk through the door.

Austin jumps up from the couch, immediately closing the lid on his laptop. "Would you look at this." He opens his arms and bends down to greet Cora and Luke. "Who are these kids? They're so big."

Cora throws herself into Austin's arms, which breaks my heart. We looked at pictures of him last night so I was sure she hadn't forgotten him and wouldn't be scared. She rests her head on his shoulder, and he kisses her hair while he rocks her in a giant hug.

Then he sets her down and extends a hand to Luke. "Hey, little man. Do we shake hands now or what?"

Luke chuckles, but I can see he's a little more nervous than Cora was. He doesn't say anything but sort of leans close to Austin, who wraps him in his arms. "It's been a minute, man. It's okay if you kind of forgot me."

But then, Austin sniffles. He steps away from Luke and covers his face with his hand. He dramatically flops to the floor, pretending to be hurt. "You don't remember your favorite uncle. It's okay, guys. I'm not hurt."

Luke flops onto the floor and hugs Austin, reassuring him, "I remember. I remember."

As much as I doubt I'll try the same technique to get Luke past his speaking anxiety, I'm impressed at how effective it is.

Once everyone is standing and the hugs are done, I send the kids to the bathroom to wash their hands so I can give Austin a hug of my own.

"Hey, man. Amazing to see you." I clap him hard, and he hugs me back before motioning his arms around the place. "Cute house, adorable neighborhood. I can see why you left the city. This is a whole change of pace."

I nod. "Star Falls is starting to feel like home. You want to go out for dinner? Gracie's brother owns the best Italian restaurant here in town."

"Gracie?" He cocks his chin and grins at me. "Is that her name? Tell me all about her. And yeah, I'm down for Italian. Luke still love pasta?"

"More than anything," I confirm. "I should call and see if we need a reservation."

When the kids come back to the living room, I

empty their backpacks and send them upstairs to play so Austin and I can talk.

"Fifteen minutes," I tell Luke. "Watch your sister for fifteen minutes. I'm going to try to get us a reservation at Benito's. You feel like going out for pasta?"

"Is Gracie going to come?" he asks.

Austin shoots me a look that says everything.

"Nah, bud. Gracie's working tonight. But we'll see her this weekend, I'm sure. I want her to meet Uncle Austin. Go on now. Fifteen minutes."

Once the kids are upstairs, Austin drops onto the couch. "I see the kids like her. What's she do?"

"You're not going to believe this," I say, kicking off my shoes. "She's a fucking artist. A tattoo artist. She's amazing. Creative, colorful. Bold. I just… She's incredible. She really is something."

Austin is quiet for a second. "I'm happy for you, Ryder," he says. He walks to the kitchen, where pictures colored and signed by Cora, Luke, and Gracie decorate the refrigerator. "This is her?" he asks, pointing to the menu from Benito's enhanced by the pair of swallows she drew at lunch three months ago.

I nod. "That's her."

Austin whistles. "That's talent." He picks up a small note that has a train sketched on it. A handmade card crafted from textured paper with a small, highly stylized image of a boy riding a train into Mrs. Lee's classroom. "She did this? For Luke?"

I grin. "Yeah." There are little signs of Gracie's presence in our lives everywhere. "They say opposites attract, but we're not opposites," I tell him.

"Does she want kids? Has she ever been married?"

"No to the marriage thing. I don't know about kids. That's one thing we haven't talked about. It seems like putting the cart before the horse when we haven't even had an overnight date yet."

Austin wanders to the art and looks closer. "You weren't even like this with Elizabeth," he says softly. "Not even when things were good."

"I know." I join him in the kitchen to pour us something to drink. "I'm happy. I like her and…I don't know. Since I have my kids already, I don't feel in a rush to figure out what this is. If it could be forever. It's so different dating women now, you know?"

Austin slaps his hands together and crows out a laugh. "God, remember that one woman? She wanted to meet your kids on the first date?"

"Correction," I tell him. "She wanted my kids to try calling her Mama Colleen on the first date just to see if she could imagine herself being their stepmom someday."

"I don't get women," Austin says.

I know better than to poke that sleeping bear. But still, I'm concerned. "You doing okay?"

Austin still doesn't talk about the one who got away. People do some shady-ass shit, and when you're a trusting, sweet guy with loads of money, you can make some bad choices. Or get tricked into making bad choices. Either way, Austin brought it up, so I feel like it's fair game to at least ask.

"I feel better than I have in a long time," he says excitedly. "Still not dating, but…"

That's probably as much as he'll say on the topic, so I move on.

"You want a beer?"

Austin shakes his head. "Just water."

When we sit back down on the couch, Austin's attitude has shifted. He doesn't seem nearly as excited as he did.

"I'm glad you're happy," he says. "So, you think it's serious with Gracie?"

I nod. "Hope so. Think so. But you know, we haven't really dated. I don't know how to date a woman without babysitters and family around. But in time, I hope it all happens for us. That's one of the craziest parts about this. She doesn't push. Never makes me feel guilty. Never puts her needs above the kids, but doesn't act like a martyr about it either. I always know where I stand with her. I'm happy."

"I want that for you. I do."

I'm not sure why the mood in the room has changed, but I want to hear more about what's going on for him. "So, tell me everything. Catch me up. Why the visit? How's your mom? We've got less than fifteen minutes before somebody's going to want Uncle Austin to play trains."

He chuckles and leans back against the couch. "I don't want to burst your Star Falls bubble," he says.

"But I came here hoping I could talk you into moving home. Sounds like the girlfriend complicates that."

Move home? I don't know why I'd do that now. If I'd never met Gracie, there'd be nothing other than the great food and quaintness of this small town to keep me here. And that's a lot, but not enough to build a life around.

He's right. Gracie is the reason I feel at home in Star Falls. But still, I'm curious what Austin has in mind.

"Why do you want me to move back?" I ask. "What's going on in Columbus?"

Austin sighs and leans back against the couch. "I'm done with the corporate shit, Ryder. I'm happy with the money, but the work I do every day is just… I don't care anymore. Maybe it's me getting older, but… I've applied for a management spot three times over the last year."

I nod, remembering two of the times he'd tossed his name in the ring. "Well, the first time you were passed over…"

"Right. Because they hired someone outside they'd been trying to recruit away from our biggest competitor for a year. Fine. But these last two times? Ryder, something isn't working for me anymore. My numbers are good, but my heart's not in it. That's basically what they said when they let me know I didn't get either of the last two promotions. I'm good at what I do, just not good enough for a corner office."

I rake a hand through my hair. "That's rough, man. Corporate bullshit. I can't pretend I know anything about it. You need to vent about teachers having affairs with each other, I might be able to help. But this..." I shrug. "I'm sorry. So, what, you're thinking about leaving your job?"

I'm not sure what this has to do with me, or me moving back to Columbus. I can't imagine what he needs that I can help him with.

"Here's where you come in," he says, getting excited. He leans forward and props his hands on his knees. "I want to start a business, Ryder. Something that I'm passionate about. Something that means more to me than just managing people's money."

"Okay. Do you have a business plan? Investors? What do you want to do?"

He gets up and starts pacing the floors. "Yeah, I'm in the final stages now. I want to start a franchise of gyms for kids. But not just gyms. Sports academies. Where do kids go to learn, really learn, how to play sports?"

"School, local teams, park districts. Private camps and stuff." I think of the aquatic center and how few classes they have for kids.

"Exactly," he says, getting excited. "There's no national brand in the space. No company that parents immediately think of when they are looking for a place to send their kids to learn everything. Ice skating, swimming, football, tennis..."

"I see the merit in the idea. I mean, I'd take my kids to a place like that if I could afford it. But if it hasn't been done before, there's got to be a reason why there's no one dominating that space in the market."

Austin's pacing faster, talking almost more quickly than I can believe. "There are three problems facing a brand trying to break into this space." He starts listing things off on his fingers, like real estate and capital and technical details that I'm sure fill out a business plan someplace on that laptop of his.

"My vision is to start small. Come up with a simple, scalable model. I want every kid who goes to T-ball when they're four to grow up in our facilities. Sees his little buddy playing soccer and wants to try it. Little Cora sees her friends bowling, next week she tries bowling. Think instead of Chuck E. Cheese for kids parties, they come to The Gym."

"That's the name?" I ask. "The Gym?"

"The name is still a work in progress, but think about it, Ryder. It has potential, right?"

I nod, thinking through all the ways a business like that could fail. "Are you going to buy or build the facilities?"

"We'll start with whatever we can get quickly. My plan is to bring in food and retail to support all the costs. Imagine a gym with a food court. No more needing to stop for dinner before class or a game. Mom and Dad can eat healthy adult food at any upscale dining place right inside the gym. All under one roof. We'll have childcare facilities and an entire section of the gym dedicated to athletes who need accommodations. Adapted swings, ramps. We'll bring in sponsors who want the good PR for donating gear and supporting the vision. We'll offer packages and scholarships so all kids who want to play can afford to play."

I applaud Austin's initiative, but this sounds like a big dream with very little chance of making it in the real world. "Have you thought this through?" I ask. "You're willing to give up your job to make this happen?"

He nods. "Ryder, I've secured a third of the start-up capital I need to break ground on a location in Columbus. If things go as planned, we'll open the first gym in less than three years. That's if we have to build. If I can rent a space to launch, we could be live in a matter of months."

I shake my head. "I'm impressed, man. Excited. If this is your dream, then I know you'll make it a reality."

"That's where you come in," he says. "Ryder, I came here to ask you to run the business. I'm making so much money at my job right now even just staying in my position, I can afford to pay you and cover health insurance costs for the kids. For the next year or so while I keep working, you can run the business. Be my right hand. In three years, you can be director of coaching. Shit, you can name your title, and I'll throw in a shareholder stake if you want."

I can't believe what I'm hearing. My best friend is offering me a chance to do something I love without the grind of teaching. To move home and work with him on his dream. I'm touched and humbled. Excited and scared.

"There's only one thing…" I tell him. "Gracie."

"That might not be the problem you think it is," he

says, a childlike grin lighting up his face. "So, you heard about what happened to Olson today? Levi Olson of the Cyclones?"

I shake my head. "The only drama I'm aware of that happened today is what Aiden, this fuckface in fourth grade, said to Luke at recess."

Austin drops beside me on the couch and claps his hands excitedly. "Levi Olson ran into some kind of trouble and left the Cyclones. Word is he's coming back to Star Falls to lie low for a while. He's probably dying for some good press. We reach out to him, get him on board as a sponsor, and bam. The missing piece we need to fulfill the last of the funding. And maybe we could start in Star Falls, Ryder. Maybe you stay here and don't move to Columbus. Scout a site for a first location right here in Olson's own backyard."

I'm not so sure about that. "Is a guy who was cut from an NFL team the guy you want supporting kids sports? What did he do?"

Austin waves away my fears with a hand. "It's probably some stupid shit. But a little time away forgives everything. Talent like that won't go to waste. The league knows that. They're probably just trying to apply pressure or get ahead of some PR nightmare before it blows up. Worst-case scenario, if he has to prove that he's ready to go back on the field, there's no better redemption story than spending his time on this while he's here. He doesn't ever have to have contact with kids, Ryder. A couple social media posts, a few photo ops. A little exposure from a guy like that could go a long, long way."

I'm not sure how I feel, but it's impossible not to get swept up in Austin's passion. "I like the idea of staying here in Star Falls and opening a small starter gym first," I say, starting to get into it. "Lower real estate costs, lower taxes. And a wealth distribution not unlike the city. There's upper class and lower, so it could be a good test case for expanding into bigger cities and more locations."

"Exactly," he says. "I was pretty stoked about having you back in Columbus, but I could live with you working out here. I can work remotely from my job once in a while anyway. I'll come out here once a month and work with you, handle anything that needs to be done on-site. And that'll give you time to figure things out with your lady. And if shit goes south, you can move back to Columbus. Or anywhere you want, man. We could go national with this. You want to move to LA to be near your sister—"

"Uh, thanks, but no. I'm allergic to celebrities."

He laughs, and at that point, our fifteen minutes are more than up. Luke and Cora thunder down the stairs, demanding dinner and playtime, respectively. I'm honestly surprised we got so much time to ourselves.

I pick up Cora and make that call to Benito's to see if we can get a table for dinner. While Austin gets on the floor to check out Luke's newest train, he gives me a look. "You'll think about it?"

Like anything that's going to impact the lives of my

kids, I need to know everything that's involved, but I admit, I'm more than intrigued. "Yeah. We'll go over the details, and we'll talk more before you go back."

I am pretty sure that this is the last sign I've been looking for. A dream job working for my best friend, doing something in a place I want to be. I want to say yes now, but before I make any future-altering plans, I don't just want to think about it. I want to talk to Gracie.

CHAPTER 16
GRACIE

MY LAST CLIENT of the night is a sweetie, but it's after nine by the time I peel off my gloves. My plan is to head home and shower and then quickly meet up with Ryder for whatever he has planned. I should be exhausted after a full day of work, but as soon as I grab my purse and keys, I realize it's happening.

My first real date alone with Ryder.

Excitement buzzes through my system while nervous energy has me feeling a little worried. I don't know what he has planned, but this feels big.

Time alone.

A real date.

After a little over three months, we know each other.

The second I'm in my car, I drop him a text.

Leaving work. Home to shower then I'll meet you at your place?

I add a string of fire and heart emojis, hit send, and

head home to shower. Thankfully, my parents are playing cards with friends tonight. They should be out for at least another hour or two.

After I shower, I pick a pair of jeans with a few well-placed shreds in them and a tank top that pops against my skin tone. I wear a slouchy black sweater that falls over one shoulder, revealing the face of the family tree tattoo. I zip into some ankle boots and shake out my hair. Once I drag some product through my hair, I toss it around so the natural waves give it some shape, and I finish my look with eyeliner and a little blush. I leave my lips glossy and check my reflection in the mirror.

I look flushed and happy, but that small worry tightens my belly. What if Ryder really wants to have sex? Expects it? I mean, fuck, I would. If I didn't have this medical test in a few days, I'd pounce on him the second I climbed into his car.

I start to worry that I should have told him sooner… prepared him that I'm having a test and have to abstain. But I don't know if he's going to want to go someplace we can be alone or if he really wants to make this a "date."

When I arrive, I knock softly at the door. Ryder answers within seconds and draws me to his chest in a hug.

"You look stunning," he says into my hair. "God, Gracie."

I hold him close, pressing my face to a long-sleeved black shirt with a green pattern of leaves and vines in it.

He's wearing regular blue jeans, and when I breathe him in, he smells divine. Better than I remember. Like fresh laundry and musky cologne and him. It's impossible to describe the way he smells, and I've been up close and personal with a lot of different people. His skin smells like sunshine and dry leaves, an enticing scent to match an enticing man.

He pulls back and takes my hand. "Do you want to meet Austin?"

I nod and follow Ryder into the living room, where a really attractive guy with muscles for days and sandy blond hair reaches out his hand. If a reality show lifeguard and male model produced offspring, that child wouldn't grow up to be as hot as Austin.

"Gracie," he says warmly. "So good to meet you. I can hardly get the kids and Ryder to talk about anything else."

I shake his hand and smile. "Great to meet you too."

"I met your brother Benito last night. Oh my God, that food."

I grin and nod. "He's an asshole, but he can cook."

Ryder grabs a jacket and pockets his keys and wallet. "Anything comes up, just text. You know where we'll be."

We head out together, our fingers tightly laced. "So," I murmur, "Austin knows where we're going. Feel like sharing with your date?"

"Quite the opposite," he says, grinning. "Climb in, please."

He holds the passenger door open for me, and I get into a car that is noticeably absent of car seats. I breathe deeply. "It smells like Icy Rain in here," I tease, making up a scent to match the heavy smell of car fragrance. "Car detailed, no car seats… What do you have planned, Mr. Cooper?"

"Well, the car seats are just practical. I put them in Austin's car in case he has any emergencies while we're out. Much faster than waiting for me to get home and move the seats."

He has a point there, but it strikes me then how different his date prep was from mine.

He climbs behind the wheel, and I reach for his arm. "Thank you," I tell him. "For going to all this trouble."

He leans across the seats to kiss me. "None of this is trouble. It's effort. There's a big difference." His lips are soft and sweet on mine. Tasting, lingering, but not probing. The hunger and drive for more isn't there. This is a sweet kiss. Loving and reassuring. "There's no amount of effort I wouldn't go to for you, Gracie."

He settles in his seat and pulls something out of the pocket of his jacket. It's a child's scarf.

"I'm not cold," I say, confused.

Ryder laughs, and the sound is real and loud. "I don't have a sexy kit like yours," he teases. "This was the best blindfold I could find on short notice."

"Blindfold?" I ask, raising an eyebrow.

"Yeah," he says. "You've lived in this town your whole life. If this is the only chance I get to surprise you, it's not going to be much of a surprise if you see exactly where we're headed."

I nod and wrap the scarf around my eyes, then I lean back in my seat. At this hour, I can't imagine what he has planned, but I don't have long to wait. When the car finally stops, he tells me to wait.

"I'll come and open the door."

The night air chills my cheeks when he opens the door and takes my hand. "Blindfold stays on, please."

I chuckle and grip his hand tighter. "Should I be afraid right now?"

He takes both my hands and leads me with his voice and his slow steps less than fifteen paces. I can peek under the scarf and see sidewalk, so I'm not too concerned I'm going to fall, but I don't hear anything that hints at where we are. A club? A restaurant? A mall?

I hear a click and then a door open, after which Ryder helps me over a small threshold and then closes a door behind me. Then he gently turns my head and unties the scarf.

"Okay, now this is going to take a little explaining, so bear with me."

When I open my eyes, I know exactly where we are. We are in a suite at the Star Falls Inn. A gorgeous local bed-and-breakfast. I see things scattered all over the room, but Ryder is excitedly tugging me toward the small desk to our left.

"Okay," he says. "This is speed dating single dad

style. But not with, like, different people. With different dates. Date number one…"

On the small desk is a bouquet of flowers. Soft blue hydrangeas mixed with bright orange tiger lilies, white roses, and beautiful leafy greens. "Flowers for our first date," he explains.

Then he hurries me to the next "station." On the hotel dresser, he's collected single-serving size bottles of wine. There is a small plate of tasty-looking seeded crackers, olives, and fruit spread out. "Hold, please." He runs to the mini-fridge and pulls out a tiny cheesecake. "Date number two—drinks and apps, plus dessert."

"Date number three is the big one," he says, a boyish grin on his face. He drags me to the big TV, where he fumbles for a moment before pulling up a rom-com. "The 'come to my place and watch a movie' date."

The last place he brings me is to the bed. Sitting on top of a pristine white duvet is an envelope with my name scribbled on it. "Open it," he says, his voice soft.

I reach across the pillows and grab the envelope. Inside is a piece of plain white paper folded into a card. On the front, Ryder has drawn some absolutely hilarious stick people in four sizes. Two kids, one man, and I assume the stick figure with the long waves of black hair is me. Inside, the card reads,

Tonight is about getting to know you better, nothing more. No pressure. Just great conversation, old movies, and a lot of snacks no little kid is going to steal.

Yours,

Ryder

I put the card back in the envelope and face him. "When did you have time to do all this?"

He chuckles. "Austin's a good friend. He helped and took the kids to the hotel pool while I set all this up earlier."

"You…" I rise up on my toes and touch his cheek. His face is smooth where he's shaved for our date, and I trail my fingers along the supple skin. "You did so much. No one's ever done anything like this for me before."

I want to look back at the flowers and the snacks and the movie queued up and ready to watch, but I can't tear my eyes from his face.

"No one's ever treated me the way you do," he murmurs.

He lifts my face to his and kisses me, long and slow and sweet. I hum and sigh at the ease of it all. We're not rushing. No one to hide from here. Heat pools between my legs, and I know I'm going to struggle with this huge comfy bed and hours of privacy ahead of us.

He pulls his lips from mine just far enough to whisper against my mouth. "We're finally alone."

"Ryder, I…" I swallow, my throat feeling like sandpaper. "I want all of this," I tell him. "Fuck, I want all of you. But I can't. Not tonight."

Ryder looks concerned, his brows knitting together. "Are you okay, Gracie? What's going on?"

I'm not sure I want to tell him everything. How can I

open up about my health and not completely obliterate the mood?

"Hey." He loops his arms around my waist, and I rest my back against his front. Our eyes meet in the bathroom mirror. He's smiling and nodding at me. "Whatever it is, I can handle it. You don't feel ready for sex for any reason, it's off the table. I'll shut the door, and we won't come back in here. Unless, I mean, you have to pee or something."

I chuckle and shake my head. It's nice looking at him this way. Seeing us together makes something shift in my chest. I'm seeing us the way the world does. Like a couple. Two people bonded and together. There for each other. Ryder literally has my back right now. And I'm not sure there's ever going to be a good time to tell him everything.

So I watch his face and explain. "I have a gynie appointment Tuesday," I say. "I have to have a test done, so I can't have intercourse until after the test is over. Bad timing," I say sadly. "When I found out we were going to have this date, I thought about rescheduling the test. But they schedule based on my cycle, so..."

"Why would you reschedule? If you need the test, my God, get it done, Gracie." His face is worried, his lips drawn thin. "Is there any chance something is wrong? Is this a routine thing?"

I nod. "There's a chance I won't be able to have kids, or if I can, that it won't be easy. I..."

This is where it gets to be impossible. Do I share

everything? On our first official date?

"Gracie," he says, turning me to face him. "Don't worry about telling me. I want to know everything there is to know about you. I don't care about sex tonight or what date this is. I am falling for you. So if it affects you, it matters to me."

I take his hand and lead him to the table by the first date station. I hold his hands and give him the simplest version of the story. "I've only been pregnant once," I tell him. "It was an accident. I hooked up with a guy, and he's totally out of the picture now. Not a part of my life. He ghosted me, actually, and it was a pretty horrific and shameful experience." My face is lowered as I tell him about the miscarriage.

"Holy shit," Ryder says. He gets up from the table and pulls me close in a hug. "First of all, I wanna know the name of this fucking douchebag."

I laugh. "Get in line. My pops has already decided he's willing to spend his retirement years in prison serving time for assault."

"I can't let your dad do it alone," he says, holding me tight. "There are no words, Gracie. What you went through. My God. You're so strong."

He holds me, and a few tears of gratitude wet the front of his shirt. I knew deep down that he would be supportive and understanding. But now…

"Ryder." I lift my face to look at him. "I'm sorry to ruin the mood."

"Stop." He holds a finger to my lips. "Never, ever apologize for being honest with me. I want to know the truth, Gracie. After everything I've been through, I can handle whatever it is that's happening with you. What I can't handle is lies. If you need me to be there when you have the tests, I can try to..."

I shake my head. "No, it's okay. My mom is taking me, and I promise, if I need anything, I'll let you know."

"Are you afraid?" he asks.

I sigh. "Honestly, yeah. But not of the test or pain or anything. I'm afraid what I'll feel like if I know for sure I can't have kids of my own. My family is so big and so close. It'll be weird thinking that this is it. Just me. Living with my parents until I die."

Ryder chuckles. "You know, Gracie, I doubt that you have to live with your parents just because you don't have kids. You can get a place of your own. Or, you know, move in with a boyfriend. Or husband. If someday you were to have one of those."

I nudge him in the ribs. "You think maybe someday I might have one of those, huh? Maybe?"

"I'll make you your own key," he says, his voice thick with emotion. "No hiding it under the mat."

I can't reply to that. Just grab him and hold him tight. I scratch my nails along his back and breathe in the scent of him. There could be a real future with this man. A future where we love each other, and it doesn't matter whether or not the children in our lives came from my body. Together, we could make a new branch on the family tree.

He pulls me toward the bed. "Sit," he says. "I'm

gonna get all our stuff together. Let's get this date started."

I kick off my boots and tug off my sweater, then climb onto the bed on top of the covers. Ryder comes back from the bathroom with a hand towel and the massage oil and sets that beside the bed. Then he gathers all the snacks and drinks, toes off his boots, and climbs on the bed beside me.

"So," he says, "your choice, Gracie. Where do we start?"

I point to the massage oil. "Can we use that without…"

He nods. "You don't have to tell me twice. We follow the doctor's rules."

I take the bottle, peel away the plastic safety seal, and flip open the cap. "But there is a whole lot that doesn't break the rules, right?"

"So, so much." His voice is low and heavy with promise. His eyes sparkle, and he nods at the massage oil. "Do you have ideas? Because I am happy to make suggestions…"

"You've done a lot of work on this date already," I tell him. "Let me take over."

I stand up off the bed and strip off my jeans and top. He watches me climb back onto the bed in nothing but a nude-colored lace bra and matching panties. I raise a brow at him and wait. "And?" I insist. "Are those clothes staying on?"

He takes the hint and leaps off the bed. Unzipping his pants, he wriggles out of them, pulls off his socks, then unbuttons his shirt and sets it all on a chair. He thumbs the waistband of his boxer briefs. "Leave these?"

"For now," I say. "On your back, please."

He climbs back into the bed and sits upright, propped against the pillows. I turn down the lights so only the bright image from the TV lights the room.

CHAPTER 17
RYDER

BY THE GLOWING light coming from the TV, I stare into her beautiful gray eyes.

"I want more of this," I tell her. "More of you."

"How late can we stay?" she purrs seductively.

"You can stay all night if you want," I tell her. "I should get home before the kids wake up. I prepaid for the room, so anything you need, just charge to it and sign my name before you leave."

She smiles at me, and I want this forever.

"Do you think this could be more?" I ask. "I want it all with you, Gracie. I don't care if this is fast. We've known each other over three months. You know my kids. This isn't just…a fling for you, is it?"

She bristles at the word, and I immediately feel like a dick.

"If this is a fling, it'll go down in history as the longest, slowest fling ever."

I laugh and push the hair back from her face. Even

with us just lying here facing each other, she's the most perfect thing I've ever seen. "I just..."

It occurs to me that lying in bed half dressed, spilling my heart out is probably the worst time to tell her about Austin's business and the job he offered me. But maybe it's also the best time.

If Grace doesn't feel the same way, like this is more than I expected and everything I want, maybe I should take the opportunity now to go back to Columbus.

Before things go any further.

Before I get my heart broken. Again.

"So, my friend Austin," I start, trying to ease into it. "He came for the weekend to talk to me about a business he wants to start."

"Yeah?" she snuggles deeper under the covers but then looks like she's thinking. "Want some cheesecake?"

"Oh, hell yeah," I say. I forgot we have snacks and treats, but the real treat is watching Gracie walk around in nothing except her sexy underwear to bring everything to the bed.

"Plates," I say, banging my forehead with the heel of my hand. "I knew I forgot something."

"Who needs plates?" she asks, sticking a fork into the creamy delight. She scoops a big hunk of the fresh strawberry swirl. "You got this from Taste, didn't you? Over by the aquatic center?"

I nod. "You know Star Falls."

"It's home," she says. "Always has been. Always will be."

That hits me hard, and I wonder if she would ever be open to moving. To going anyplace else. If what this is could be enough to convince to her leave if I did.

My appetite is starting to die, but I slice a huge bite of cheesecake with the tines of my fork and scoop it up. "Have you ever wanted to live in a big city?"

She lifts one of those perfect brows and licks the last bit of cream from her fork. "No. Everything I love is here."

I nod and look down at my fork. I slip the bite into my mouth and…fuck. I mean, it's freaking good. Everything about Star Falls is better than I expected.

"I always thought kids who grew up in small towns had big-city dreams." I laugh to try to cover my own feelings of anxiety about the topic. "I mean, isn't there a whole genre of movies dedicated to that?"

She matches my humor with a smile so beautiful I want to put aside the dessert and kiss her again. "Yeah, of course. A lot do. But when you have such a big, tight family like I do… I don't know." She's quiet for a minute. "Sometimes I think Vito isn't happy here. His life hasn't turned out the way he planned, and I mean, whose has? That's adulthood. But I wonder if someday we'll wake up and he'll just announce that he's leaving."

I nod. "How would your parents take it? His moving, let's say, really far away. Like my sister in Los Angeles?"

She raspberries a breath through her lips and shakes her head. "No one in my family is the LA type." But then she's quiet for a moment. Really thinking about it. "God, it'd be hard," she admits. "It'd be hardest on my mom and dad. They'd worry every day they couldn't run down the street and check on their kids."

I don't say anything to that, and she finally fills up the silence.

"It does sound a little smothering when I say it out loud."

"No, no," I reassure her. "That's not what I'm getting at. I've been thinking about all this ever since we moved here. I wanted a fresh start, and I am falling hard for Star Falls…"

She leans over and plants a kiss on my shoulder when I say that.

"I just wonder how parents make those decisions. Like if I stay here with Luke and Cora, and then someday they want to leave? Would I give them better opportunities if I moved to, say, New York?"

She widens her eyes. "That's a leap."

"I know. And I'm not saying I've considered it, but…" I decide to get it all out. Put my cards on the table and see how Gracie reads them. "Austin wants to start a business," I tell her. "He asked me to move back to Columbus and run it for him."

"Whoa, whoa. Back up." She doesn't give me the brow, but the look of utter shock on her face makes me feel sick. She looks like she thinks I've betrayed her. "You're thinking about leaving?"

I lean back against the pillow. "No. I mean, I honestly don't know what to do. I want to do the right thing for my kids above everything else. But I'm not enjoying teaching the way I did before. I have been thinking about all the choices I've made. Where I live. Who I keep around me. All of it." I look at her, trying to gauge how she feels, but she is stone silent, her face completely unreadable.

The next words she says cracks a crater in my heart.

"I need a glass of water. Excuse me." She gets up from the bed and walks into the bathroom. Then she returns and climbs back into bed, holding a glass of water.

"Are you okay? Did I do something wrong?"

All of a sudden, there are tears in her eyes. "I just…" She wipes a tear that falls down her cheek, and she shakes her head. "I can't believe you'd leave. I know it's really early, but I'm attached, Ryder. To you. To the kids. I…" She rubs a hand across her face and sniffs hard. "This isn't just a fling to me. I am falling for you."

I reach for her, opening my arms, and she climbs across the bed and cuddles against my chest.

"I feel the same way," I tell her. "Since the day I set eyes on you, I knew there was something about you. I think it was your coffee addiction, your bossiness, and your right eyebrow."

She lifts her face to glare at me. "It's not an addiction. It's a habit I can break if I need to, but come on."

I kiss her forehead. "So, you're not going to deny being bossy and having eyebrows that basically have their own personalities?"

She grimaces but then smiles. "You know me well.

And I want to get to know you better, Ryder. I want more of these times. Is that selfish? Am I pressuring you to stay?"

I don't know the answer to that. What I don't want to do is make a mistake because of my feelings for a woman. I've done that. And while my marriage to Elizabeth wasn't what I wanted it to be, I have two kids who are part of my soul now. I can't afford to make the same mistakes again. It's not just me they will affect.

"It's not pressure," I tell her. The light from the TV shifts into sleep mode. The logo of the inn pops up in plain stark-white letters, casting a slightly ghostly glow on our faces. I feel colder and tuck the blankets up to our chests. "You're just being honest with me. That's one of the things I love about you. I always know where I stand."

She nods. "Yeah, but you should be excited about your work. Or at least satisfied with your choice. You shouldn't waste energy wondering what if. So, what's going on with the high school? Is it being part time or is it not coaching yet? Do you think you'd feel the same way if you were teaching back in Columbus?"

"I don't know," I admit. "It's been three years now that I've been away. And coming back to a new school seemed like the right idea. New faces, no old memories to drag me into the past. But nothing about it feels the same as it did before I had kids. I want to work—I mean, fuck, I need to work. I've been off longer than I ever imagined I would be. But the idea of doing something else...the idea of running a business with my best friend is exciting, Gracie."

I tell her about Austin's gym idea, and even though I don't know a lot of details, she agrees it sounds like an amazing opportunity. Something that would be perfect for me. Great for the kids.

"Austin said he'd consider launching here in Star Falls, but I don't know if he meant it. But what if it doesn't work?" I ask. "What if I end up accepting the job, but then I need to move to Columbus in three or six months anyway? It's a ton of risk. I mean, my god. I trust Austin with my kids, but trusting him with my financial future?"

She frowns. "So many start-ups don't make it even when they are well-funded. Having a good idea and great people isn't enough. I didn't have anyone else to consider when I started The Body Shop. If it failed, it wouldn't hurt anyone, except it would sting a little for me."

I nod. I wish it was easier to know I'm doing the right thing. I wish I could just follow my heart and not have to worry about the lives and futures that depend on my making the right choices.

"I can't believe I'm responsible for making a choice this big and there's no clear path," I say. "I mean, following my heart felt a lot simpler when I was in college. Now? How do I look at Luke and Cora and tell them we're moving again? Or in six months if the business fails and I have to...I don't know what, Gracie. It's scary."

She looks into my eyes. "I don't know if I could lose you. And I don't know how to tell you to make this decision. All I can say is every decision I've ever made, I made with my heart. Not my head." She sighs. "And fuck, those haven't all been good. But at least I knew I went with what I wanted, Ryder. If you deny yourself what you think you want, even if you think it's for the good of your kids, don't you think that could lead to resentment someday? Not toward your kids, of course, but toward the world, toward life? I don't know if I could make a good choice if I felt backed into a corner."

"I have options, though," I tell her. "If I take the job with Austin and it doesn't work out, I can probably go back to Columbus and teach there. But then we're right back to where we started. Where do I go and why?"

She nods. "I'm going to make this really simple for you, because what I want is easy. My life is here, Ryder. But there's more to consider than that. You have other people counting on you."

I lift her face to mine and kiss her. She tastes like strawberries and cheesecake, and it's the best damn thing I've ever tasted. I can't imagine leaving her any more than I can imagine letting her down.

"But," she continues, "Columbus isn't that far away. We could do the long-distance thing for a while."

The crater in my heart fills immediately at her words. The fact that she would consider a long-distance relationship means something. This is a woman I can make decisions around. Make decisions with. Most of all, I need to make decisions in my life because she's in it.

"I can't take you from this place," I tell her. "Benito's restaurant. The Body Shop. Your family. Everyone you've known. There's still a chance it could work here in Star Falls. Austin has some ideas."

As we talk about logistics, I start yawning. I'm exhausted and should probably get some sleep before I head home.

"You going to sleep here or leave now?" she asks.

"I'll set an alarm to get home before the kids wake up. Do you want to tell your parents where you are, so we don't have a repeat?"

She shakes her head and tosses the towel aside to curl up with me. "No. They know I'm with you. I told them there is a chance I wouldn't come home until tomorrow."

She snuggles against me, and I stroke her hair, when a thought occurs to me. "Gracie, do you or your brothers know anything about Levi Olson?"

Gracie sits upright, clutching the blanket to her chest. She's glaring at me, a wild, angry look on her face. "What do I know about Levi Olson?"

"Yeah. By the look on your face, I'd say it's nothing good."

She cackles in the darkest way. "Not a damn thing."

"Austin heard he was a hometown boy who's coming back to Star Falls. One of the ideas he brainstormed for keeping me in Star Falls was reaching out to the guy to see if he wants to sponsor or in some way affiliate with the kids gym."

"Levi Olson, sponsoring a kids gym? You've got to be fucking kidding me. That's ripe."

"What happened?" I ask, completely confused by how pissed she seems. "Based on your answer, I'd say you know him, know him. Is he an asshole or something? I told Austin the guy might have some baggage…"

"Baggage," she says, her lips trembling. "I'll tell you what kind of baggage Levi Olson has. And then you tell me if you still want to work with him."

"What did he do to you?"

All the sleepiness of a few minutes ago has disappeared. Now I'm worried.

"If that asshole hurt you…" I say, starting to get worked up.

She blurts out the whole story then. When she's done, when it's over, she hangs her head as she sits on the edge of the bed.

"I can't do this," she says quietly. "It's taken all my strength to put myself out there again. It was hard enough that you have kids, and this is nothing against Luke and Cora, but Ryder, I can't take another heartbreak. I've been working through that, but to have Levi Olson come back to town, and to think of you courting him…"

"I won't," I promise. "I don't care what's at stake for Austin's business. That fucker hurt you, Gracie. The last thing you have to worry about is that I'm going to work with the guy. I don't do business with men who treat women like shit, and I'm guessing you're not the first woman he's done this to. Tell me how to find him. Give me his number. While Austin's in town, we'll pay him a visit."

She looks at me with doubt on her face, but when she sees I'm dead serious, she manages a weak smile. "Dad's got it covered. Ma offered to tweet about it, and Dad wants to take a mallet to his knees."

"Give me a turn with the mallet," I offer.

She sighs and folds her hands in her lap. "Maybe this is a sign, Ryder," she says. "A sign that your future is in Columbus. Maybe we shouldn't be together. What are the odds that—"

"Whoa, whoa, whoa. Back up. You think what that fucker did has anything to do with what's happening between us? The odds that an asshole ballplayer gets canned and comes running home with his tail between his legs to hide out? Pretty high, actually. Our actions always catch up to us, Gracie. Even though, for some people, it takes a while. Look. The fact that the guy is from here is the only reason why you ever met him. If he hadn't been in town for a wedding, would he have ever come through The Body Shop?"

She shakes her head. "Unlikely."

"All right. So that's small-town life. For better or worse, you know everybody, and everybody knows you. The real question is, are you going to be okay when that waste of human flesh comes back to town? Maybe we should *all* move to Columbus."

I'm not sure how's she going to react to that, but I'm surprised when she scoots closer to me. She laces her fingers through mine and squeezes. "I don't want to run from anything," she says. "Look, he didn't hurt me. Not physically. He ghosted me. Bailed on his responsibility. Was a colossal asshole, but not completely surprising. But other than make me feel like shit about myself, he is nothing to me. Not then, and not now. I'll handle it in the future. I don't want to run away from anything ever again."

I raise her hand to my lips. "I won't have anything to do with the gym if Austin insists on working with the guy. There are some good, principled men out there, Gracie. Your father is one. I'm sure your brothers are. I'm one of them too, Gracie."

"Meh," she quips. "I'm not so sure about Benito."

We both crack up, but then I take her face in my hands. "You just made a tough decision a lot easier. I'll tell Austin no. I'll be here for you when that asshole comes back to town. I'll figure out what to do with my career eventually. This matters to me, Gracie—how you feel about what I choose to do with my life. That's what a real relationship looks like."

We kiss again, but the heat isn't there. It's reassuring and loving, but we're both exhausted.

Despite everything we've talked about in this crazy hotel room, I've never felt more at home in my life.

CHAPTER 18
RYDER

I'D COME to a decision before we parted ways at the hotel early this morning, but I hadn't shared my decision with anyone, including Gracie. Not yet. I wanted to be one hundred percent certain about that decision before I told anyone.

What did I decide? I'd be fucking bananas if I quit my job to join my buddy in a new start-up. No matter how great his vision is...it may amount to nothing. I'm not a single man with no responsibilities. I don't have the luxury of taking risks that very well could affect our happiness and financial means.

Even if I were able to take a huge financial risk, there is Gracie to consider. I've barely touched the woman, but none of that matters. I know her on a different level; I don't think I know any other female in my life in quite the same way.

And in a short amount of time, I've allowed myself

to dream of future possibilities. And every single one of them includes Star Falls and Gracie.

My love for coaching and teaching will come back eventually. There's an ebb and flow to everything in life, including work. Once I get accustomed to life in Star Falls and get to know more of the people and kids, that vigor I felt before will return.

The gray cloud of grief that has been over my head for what feels like forever has started to break apart, allowing me to see things in a new light.

My life isn't over.

Gracie has shown me that.

My time for love and happiness hasn't passed.

The world is filled with possibilities.

But every single one of them is in Star Falls.

"I don't want to pressure you, man," Austin says as we stand in the park with the kids, giving them something to do this morning to burn some energy. "If you're out, I do want to start talking to some of our other friends. Maybe start looking at talent recruitment companies to get the best of the best."

I shake my head and give Cora a little boost, and I watch her ladybug-patterned sneakers kick high in the air. "I don't know," I tell him. "The idea is intriguing. I just..." I decide to tell him as little about Levi as I can. "I asked Gracie what she knows about this Olson guy, and..." I shake my head.

Austin moves around to the front of the swings to face me. "What did she say?"

"He sounds like bad news. I don't know what kind

of trouble he's in, but if you're fixed on getting a guy like him on board, you're asking for a world of trouble."

Austin looks shocked but nods. "He's out, then. Anything else stopping you?"

"This part's harder," I tell him. "I believe in this vision more than anything, but I don't want you to change your business model because of me and where I live or where I might want to live. I'm falling in love with Gracie, and I want to see where that goes. Enough that I've decided I'm going to stay put in Star Falls. This is your dream, man, and I support it even if I can't be part of it."

Austin kicks the spongy turf beneath the swings with the tip of his running shoe. "I appreciate you doing some digging on that ballplayer," he says. "That could have been a minefield I stepped right into." He looks disappointed but says, "Would you consider maybe being a consultant for the company? You can work from home and maybe come down to Columbus for a weekend when something can't be done online?"

"Really?" I ask, shocked he's still trying to find a way for me to stay part of the business.

"Heck yeah. Most things can be done online now. I really value your input, Ryder, and there's no one else I trust more than you, too. It won't take up much time, and I promise it won't interfere with your current job or life."

"I'm only working part time right now. A teacher is retiring next year, and I'll be getting his position. But I do have the rest of this school year, and my summers are free except for coaching, which includes training and practice for the next season."

"So, Gracie's the real deal, huh? You're staying put for good. You're home?"

"Yeah, she is."

"I'm happy for you, buddy. Really happy for you."

"It's just…" Cora wants off the swing, so I wait to answer the question until both my kids have climbed the ladder to the curly slide. While Luke goes down first and Cora stands at the top waiting for her turn, I explain. "My whole marriage was a lie."

Austin lowers his eyes and nods. "I know, Ryder. I can't imagine…"

I sigh. "I hope you never have to either. Every day, I tried to make things better. I tried to prove I was worth the life I had, even though, deep down, I always knew I'd never be what Elizabeth really wanted. That's the thing about Gracie. I always know what she thinks. Where she stands. I never, ever have to worry that she's giving me some bullshit."

"It's rare to find someone you trust," he says, a bitterness underlying his words. "And even when you do trust someone…"

He doesn't have to finish that thought. I don't know how badly Austin's ex fucked him over, but I know that what I went through with Elizabeth is something he can relate to. The only difference is I ended up having two kids as a permanent reminder that I wasn't enough.

But with Grace, I feel like I am enough. More than enough. I feel like I'm exactly what she wants. We're so different, and yet, we're exactly the same in the ways that matter.

Our families mean everything. Our work is important, but family comes first. Honesty and trust, directness and integrity. I know the hours she puts in helping at the shop that she doesn't get paid for. The time she spends because she wants to make a difference to her employees and her town.

She is what I want, and I believe she wants me. Where we'll be come summer or next spring or two winters from now, I don't know. But I know what we have is worth trying for. Worth putting first. Ahead of Austin's opportunity. Ahead of any lingering doubts, insecurities, or fears that might hold me back.

"She's going to win out if I have to choose," I tell Austin with a grin. "I mean, come on. Look at her. Look at you."

"I'd worry if you didn't pick her," Austin laughs. "So, I'll send text and email updates. If it's urgent or exciting, I'll call, and we'll just play it by ear week to week."

"I'd like that," I tell him. We clap hands and pull each other into a half hug. "So, what's next for you? You going to start dating or just keep your nose deep in sports stats and business plans?"

"Definitely the second," he grits out. I can tell by the tension in his voice that he's not ready to talk.

Thankfully, the kids are.

"Dad!" Luke screams. "Cora ate a piece of gum from

the slide. It was just sitting there, and I told her not to touch it, and she ate it anyway."

Austin looks like he's going to be sick, and I raise a brow at him. "Parenthood. Most exciting game you'll ever play." Then I trot over to the slide to find Cora, working her jaw on the old piece of gum. "Did you put something from the slide in your mouth?"

This is one of those moments I'm sure I'll forget in twenty years. I won't care about how many pieces of used gum my kids ate, if they cried through their naps, or whether they ate their broccoli.

"You think you could watch the kids again tonight? I need to talk to Gracie. I'll stay until the kids go down, and then I need two hours, tops."

"Ryder, who are you bullshitting? You'll last maybe five minutes. You'll be there and back in under thirty."

I smack him in the arm. "Don't be an asshole. I'm just going to talk to her."

He smirks. "Sure, man. Whatever you say."

CHAPTER 19
GRACIE

"RYDER, what are you doing here? Where are the kids?" I look out the shop window, expecting to see the kids outside, but they're not.

Ryder takes a step forward. "You alone?"

I nod. "Just finishing up some paperwork I've been putting off for far too long. What's wrong?"

He shakes his head and smiles. "Nothing's wrong, Gracie. And the kids are with Austin. He splays his palms out across my back as he pulls me closer until our bodies are fully pressed together. "I wanted to talk to you alone. It couldn't wait. I couldn't wait."

My stomach turns, and I brace myself for the news I've been dreading. We've barely had a chance to begin, and he's already going to leave. "Okay," I whisper, trying to keep the tremble out of my voice as I stare into his eyes.

"I can't leave you. I won't leave. The last few

months with you have made me feel more alive than I've felt in...well, forever really. Or at least it feels that way. I'm not ready to throw that all away to chase Austin's dream. I want to stay here, in Star Falls, and see where this goes. I'm falling for you harder and faster than I ever thought possible, and I'm not willing to walk away from this for anything, including chasing someone else's dream. I want you. I choose you."

A warmth fills my chest at his words. A sense of calm washes over me. He's staying. He's staying for me. For us. "Really?" I'm dumb struck by his decision.

I haven't had the best track record with men, and I fully expected Ryder to be no different. Heartbreak has always been the story of my life. I figured love wasn't written in my cards, and I was okay with it.

Ryder raises a hand to my face, cradling my cheek in his hand. He gazes into my eyes. "I will always choose you."

His words steal my breath and momentarily stun me. No man has ever said those words to me. No one has ever put me first. No one until now. "I love you, Ryder," I tell him, wanting nothing more than to have him in my life forever.

He smiles as he strokes his thumb back and forth against my cheek. "I love you too, Gracie." As soon as the words are out of my mouth, his lips are on mine.

He snakes his arm around my back, holding me tight until there's no space left between us. The kiss is rough, but his lips are soft.

"I want you," I breathe into his mouth, needing to feel him inside me, wanting to feel him inside me.

"Fuck," he growls against my lips, sending goose bumps scattering across my skin.

The dam of restraint breaks as I move my hands to the bottom of his shirt, pulling it upward. Ryder pulls back, breaking our kiss long enough for me to tear the shirt over his head.

His mouth comes down on mine, and he lifts me in the air, carrying me toward the back of the shop.

"What are you doing?" I ask as I wrap my legs around his middle.

"Privacy," he tells me, kicking open the door to my office and taking me inside.

I don't say another word as he sets my ass down on the desk, and I rip off my top and bra, feeling more impatient than I have in a long time. "Pants," I command as I toss my top and bra at his face, watching them hit his bare chest and fall to the floor.

Ryder smirks as he moves his hands to his zipper before yanking his jeans down to his ankles. The way he stares at me as he does this has my body aching for his touch.

"All the way." I point at his ankles, waving my finger at his pants. "No restraints."

"Baby, off the desk," he tells me, raising an eyebrow before kicking off his pants into a puddle on the floor. "Turn around. Hands on top."

A thrill runs through me at the thought of Ryder

taking me from behind and being rough instead of his usual sweet.

I do as I'm told, hopping down from the desk, placing my palms flat on the top, facing away from him, and shaking my ass in an open invitation.

A second later, Ryder's hands are at the waistband of my leggings, ripping them down my legs. But he doesn't take them all the way off. "I prefer you restrained," he whispers in my ear with his front plastered against my bare back.

I shiver, thinking of being tied up and Ryder having his way with me. That isn't what this was, but my mind drifts there as his mouth finds the tender skin of my neck and his hands explore the rise of my hips and swell of my ass.

I drop my head forward and close my eyes, focusing on every sensation as he touches and kisses my body.

This isn't slow. This isn't making love.

This is pure need. Total want.

Ryder's warm lips and soft tongue blaze a trail across my back to my shoulder. I stick out my ass, rubbing it against his hard cock.

"Ryder," I moan.

"What, baby?" he asks against my skin.

"I need you."

He slides his hand across the front of my hip and nestles it between my legs, finding my wetness and my clit. His fingertips are gentle but hit the perfect spot. "You want this?" he purrs against my ear, sending shock waves through my system as his finger circles my clit.

I ache to be stuffed, pounded into by him, as his fingers work their magic, driving me closer to an orgasm. Without my having to beg, Ryder lines up his cock to my opening and pushes inside, filling me completely.

I arch my back, adjusting to the sweet bite of his deliciously large length and girth.

Ryder's arm comes around my middle to palm my breast, while his other hand works my clit in perfect precision.

All thoughts leave my mind as he pounds into me, moving me upward and onto my tiptoes with each thrust. I'm consumed by the way he makes me feel, the pleasure he delivers.

"I love your cunt," he whispers against my ear.

I shudder with pleasure from his words as he drives into me, sending me closer to the edge. I want to spread my legs but can't. The damn leggings on the bottoms of my legs are making it impossible. But instead of struggling, I give in, taking what he's giving me.

"Ryder," I moan again, so close to the edge.

"You want to come, baby?"

"Yes," I answer, my voice hoarser than before.

"How do you want it?"

"Harder," I tell him, pushing my ass backward.

"Fuck my cock, Gracie."

I moan at the thought and do as he commands. I use my palms for leverage, slamming myself against his length, taking him as deep as I can. He works his fingers faster, pressing harder with each passing thrust of my body down his shaft.

As the orgasm starts to build, my pace quickens, trying to push myself over the edge. But I can't quite get there on my own. As if he can read my mind, Ryder flattens his fingers between my legs, swiping his hand back and forth so hard and fast, I can't stop the ecstasy from crashing over me.

My breath ceases as the air escapes my lungs, and my muscles seize from the overwhelming sensation of being pleasured. I slow my pace, wanting to savor the feeling of this moment. Ryder takes over, chasing the same pleasure as he drives me straight into another orgasm that threatens to turn my legs into jelly.

He tightens his arm around my middle, holding me to him and keeping me upright as he moans, cresting and dipping through his pleasure.

The only sounds in the shop are our heaving breathing as we try to right ourselves after something so perfect.

"Fuck," Ryder whispers.

I peer over my shoulder, still bent over the desk. "What?"

"I didn't use a condom." He gives me a pained and apologetic smile.

"It's okay. Doctor said it'll be damn near impossible for me to get pregnant without intervention."

"Damn near isn't zero," he says.

"With my luck, it's zero, Ryder. Don't worry so much."

"Okay," he says, drawing out the word. "But remember, my sperm is no joke, Gracie."

I roll my eyes at the ridiculousness of his statement. Every guy likes to think his sperm is somehow magical and superhuman.

"I think we'll be okay. I have a better chance of hitting the lottery than getting knocked up by you."

CHAPTER 20
GRACIE

SIX MONTHS *later*

"Cora, Put down the puppy, sweetheart." Ma holds open her arms to take the Chihuahua who normally snarls at everyone and everything except my ma and me from the little girl.

Cora is wearing a tiara and sparkly pink dress for her fourth birthday party. Something we've spent weeks planning.

At the moment, she has two sets of grandparents hovering over her—Ryder's parents and mine.

Ryder's parents have become really close to my family over the last few months. They drove up and stayed here at the house with my parents over Christmas, and ever since, they have kept in touch. My mother makes it impossible to lose touch unless you actively block her, but Deloris fits into Ma's gang of lady friends so well, I've overheard my parents talking about the Coopers buying a cabin near Star Falls so they can be a lot closer to their grandchildren once they retire.

When Ryder went to Columbus for Thanksgiving, he told Elizabeth's parents he was seeing someone, and they promised to try to make it to Star Falls for Christmas and then New Year's. But time after time, they made excuses not to come.

I can't say that I blame them.

Once Ryder and I started seeing each other, all the pictures he sent them either came from me or had me in them. It was probably very painful seeing someone raising their grandchildren. Someone who replaced their daughter, at least in their eyes.

Spring is in full bloom in Star Falls, and my entire family is in on the birthday celebration.

"Yeah. Yeah. Got it. Okay, thanks, sis. Love you too." Ryder slips his phone into his back pocket and loops a hand over my shoulder. "It's not official, but my sister thinks she's got him."

Austin claps his hands excitedly. "I knew it, man. I knew it. Great job, Allison."

"I'm not Allison," Cora whirls on Austin with a pout. "I'm just Cora."

He bends down to pick her up and spins her in a circle. "I know, sweetheart. I'm talking about your aunt Allison in LA. She connected me to a very famous basketball player, and I am very, very excited."

"I brought dessert. Not that we need it with that cake," Chloe says with Franco and their little girl at her side, and what I can smell is a plate of peanut butter crisps. The second I catch a whiff, I have to turn away.

"Excuse me a sec," I say and run up to my room for some fresh air.

While I'm up there, I grab Cora's birthday gift, which I'd left wrapped on my desk. I have a small gift for Luke too. I hear footsteps on the stairs, and my dad knocks lightly on the door.

"Sweetheart," he calls. "Rebecca and Daniel just pulled up."

"Thanks, Dad." I grab the gift bags and turn to face my father. "Thanks for hosting. I feel so much better doing this here."

Pops pulls me in for a hug. "This will always be your home, sweetheart. I'm just glad we can share it with more people than your idiot brothers." He starts to head downstairs, but I hold back a minute.

"I'll be right there, Pops."

I run my hands along the bedding and my drafting table. All the familiar things that make up my home. I've lived in this room and under this roof almost my entire life. Everything has changed so fast over the last year.

I savor the sounds of the dogs barking and yipping. My brothers chatting. My parents shouting back and forth through it all. And now, adding to the lovable chaos, is Ryder. His beautiful kids. More grandparents and friends. It's the family I always dreamed of. And I am so blessed to have it. And everything else that is to come.

I pop a ginger sweet into my mouth and breathe in through my nose. I've been avoiding peanut butter crisps, but until we make the big announcement, I haven't told anyone. Not even my parents. I've changed my two-cup-a-day habit to one decaf, but thankfully, I've also been working out with Ryder regularly, so Chloe just thinks I'm trying to be more fit.

I stroke my still-flat belly and wonder if everything is okay in there.

My very own little one.

Only Ryder knows I'm fifteen weeks along, but he and I plan to share the news when we're all together today.

He was worried how Elizabeth's parents would take it, but I told him this is our news. Our family. And they are part of it.

If they are unhappy, they can tell us.

They can leave.

Or they can do what any reasonable people would do and congratulate Ryder on finally finding happiness.

I hope they are as happy for us as I know everyone else will be.

Ryder and I weren't trying to conceive, but the guy must, indeed, have super swimmers. The very first time we had sex without protection, I missed a period two weeks later.

I've been terrified that something would happen, but at the same time, I know I already have everything I could ever want. If we add to the family with a child now, I will accept it and be grateful. If that doesn't happen, I will accept it and work toward finding peace.

It's all we can do. Do our best.

Push past the fears. Face the hard stuff.

With so much out of my hands, the only thing I can do is lean on the loved ones I have when the going gets rough.

It's all possible with just a few good people at your side. And I have so, so many good people.

The phone in the back pocket of my jeans buzzes with a text. I pull it out and read the message from Ryder.

Baby, if you're up in your bedroom for much longer, I'm going to come up there and...

He follows that up with a string of emojis so filthy, I grab the gifts and head down the stairs. The last thing we need is to ruin his daughter's birthday by getting it on in my bedroom.

When I reach the top of the stairs, Ma is yelling at Vito to put the dogs in the basement. Franco and Chloe are standing together talking to Austin, while Luke and Cora run to greet Rebecca and Daniel, who are just now arriving. Benito is supervising the food with Ma's friends, Bev, Sassy, and Carol, who are on hand to help serve and clean.

Ryder is the only one standing alone. His eyes are fixed on me as I come down the stairs.

I hold the banister and lift a brow at him, curious what he's thinking.

He doesn't rush to the door to meet Rebecca and Daniel. He's waiting for me.

When I reach the bottom, he clasps me in a hug and holds me close. "I love you, Gracie," he murmurs against my hair. "This is more than I ever imagined. I'm so, so happy right now. Are you?" He looks at me with such sincerity and such hope.

"I could not possibly be any happier," I tell him. And it's true.

"Gracie," a slim, beautiful woman dressed in expensive-looking black clothing, her white hair piled high in a soft topknot holds out her hands to me. "Well, it's so very nice to meet you."

"Rebecca," I say, taking her hands. "I'm so glad you're here."

She introduces me to Daniel, her husband, and we hug a little awkwardly, but Daniel seems kind. He has sad eyes, a sort of perpetual grief that hits me like a ton of bricks the moment I meet him. "Gracie, you're even more beautiful in person. Thank you for taking such good care of our grandchildren. All I ever hear about is Gracie this and Gracie that. You are a special woman to love these kids the way you do."

I've seen Elizabeth's parents on video chats before and, of course, in pictures, but as I see them for the first time in person, I can see Cora's eyes in her grandfather. Luke's slightly crooked smile bears a very clear resemblance to Rebecca's mouth. I imagine what doing something like this would be like for my parents. If they lost me and Ryder moved on to someone else. I can't imagine how painful and emotional it must be to meet me, the woman who stands in the place where their daughter should have been.

As soon as the thought hits me, tears start to well in my eyes. Rebecca immediately frowns. "Are you okay? Was it something we said?"

I shake my head. "I'm okay. Can I speak with you alone for a moment?" I look to Ryder and ask him to come with us.

By the time we reach the backyard, away from the ongoing party, I'm a lot calmer and am starting to question whether I'm overreacting.

Ryder puts an arm around my shoulders. "Everything okay?" he asks. I can tell he's concerned and a little confused. "Something happen?"

"No," I tell him. "I just don't think it would be fair to spring the news on Rebecca and Daniel. I'd like to talk to them first if you don't mind."

Ryder bites down on his lower lip but doesn't say anything. He nods at me and then kisses me on the cheek. "I'll leave you three alone."

He crosses the yard to chat up his parents, who are sitting on lawn chairs around my dad's firepit.

Rebecca immediately covers her mouth with her hand. "Gracie, perhaps we were wrong to come." She turns to her husband. "I thought we might just be in the way." She looks at me with such kindness and sadness, I want to take her in my arms and hold her. "We'll make our excuses and drive home if you prefer we not be here. This is your family now, and we're just... I am not sure we belong."

I shake my head, and tears start rolling down my cheeks. I hold up a hand. "Please, no. I'm glad you're here. You absolutely belong. Let me explain." I wipe my face and chuckle. "I'm a little emotional, as you can see. And there's a good reason."

I huddle close to them and lower my voice. "Ryder and I plan to announce to the family today while everyone is together that I'm expecting. Fifteen weeks along. I wasn't entirely sure that I could have kids, and so this is a scary blessing but an exciting one."

Rebecca's eyes shimmer with tears. "You're telling us first?" she asks, looking back at Daniel. "Before your parents? Why?"

I can hardly get the words out, but I finally do. "That's exactly why I want to share this with you first and not spring it on you. I know not everyone likes surprises." I take a deep breath and hope I'm doing the right thing. I'm sure my parents will understand if they ever find out that Rebecca and Daniel had a tiny head start on this information.

"I am so close to my parents. It's hard to explain how close. I mean, I'm over thirty years old and I still live at home because I want to." I chuckle. "That's about to change, of course, but I just cannot imagine the kind of loss you went through. Losing your daughter. I'm sure no matter how much time passes, it never gets easier...just different."

Rebecca sniffs and pulls a tissue from her bag. I rush on before any of us starts in with the waterworks.

"I feel terrified that you're going to think I'm disrespecting your daughter's life. Stepping in and taking her place. I just can't handle the thought that you lost your daughter and now you'll think that you're losing your grandchildren too. I have no intention of ever—"

Rebecca stops me with a shake of her head. "Oh, Gracie. I can see why you're the one for Ryder." She pulls me close and hugs me, patting me gently on the back. When she releases me, she holds my shoulders and looks me in the eye. "We know the things our daughter did while she was married to Ryder. We don't defend it, but we also can't hold her choices against her. All any parent wants is for their child to be happy and safe. While Ryder was good to Elizabeth, he wasn't right for her."

Daniel looks like he's near tears, and that breaks me up all over again.

"Now, listen," Rebecca says, growing stern. "No matter what, all that matters is that we are a family to these children. Luke and Cora will always be our grandchildren. Our flesh and blood. We're not as close as you are with your parents, but we are happy that they will grow up with that kind of love. I am sure if Elizabeth had lived, she would have left Ryder. I'm only hoping that he would have found you, and you would have found him, no matter what."

She holds my face between her hands and pats my cheek. "You have nothing to worry about. We are happy for Ryder, happy for you, and most of all, thrilled that Cora and Luke have you as their new mother. You've been that to them, Gracie. You've been more of a mother than our daughter had the chance to be. Accept that role. Embrace it. That's just how it should be."

She turns to Daniel and swats him playfully. "Now try to act surprised when they announce they're expecting. I don't want to get on Lucia and Mario's bad side."

"I hear Mario likes to threaten people with a mallet," I hear Daniel say as they head back toward the house.

"Only some people, dear. Better not to ask." Rebecca and Daniel lace hands and walk back inside.

Ryder is waiting for me a short distance away. He's standing near the patio doors, just watching me.

"Everything okay?" he asks, coming to meet me.

I look off into the afternoon sun. The day is cool and sunny. A light breeze plays over my hair. While I lace hands with him, we see two hummingbirds swoop down, hover near the hedge that separates our lawn from our neighbors and then fly away.

"Did you see that?" I ask. "Those hummingbirds?"

"Maybe they're a sign," Ryder says, wrapping his arms around my waist. He stands behind me and rests his chin lightly on the top of my head. He kisses my hair. "You sort things out with Rebecca and Daniel?"

I nod, and then I turn and hug him. "Let's go inside. We have a party to host."

Inside, the party is bustling. Luke is playing trains with Franco and Chloe. Austin is talking to Sassy, who is probably trying to figure out what kind of woman he likes so she can set him up.

In the yard, Cora has an absolutely ridiculous number of presents to open. Puzzles, books, clothes, sports equipment, and a brand-new sleeping bag for when she sleeps over at Nana Lucia and Papa Mario's house.

Luke gets plenty of gifts too, including a book about trains from Chloe and Franco.

I give Cora and Luke my presents last. I walk across the grass to Luke and present him with two coloring books, each one hand-drawn by me. They are identical books—one is for his sister, of course—and features pictures of many of the adventures we've shared together. There are pictures of the pasta people from Benito's menu. The kids represented by sharks taking swim lessons at the aquatic center. There are trains and pictures of Luke's school, Cora in the car going to day care. Even pictures of us together.

The last gift I have is for Cora to open. I hand the bag to Ryder for him to give his daughter, but he shakes his head and takes my hand. "Together," he says.

The entire family is hushed and watching while we walk up to Cora. She sits on a chair in the center of all of us, looking elated in her tiara and pretty dress.

"Cora," I say. "Your dad and I got you a present, but it's really something you're going to have to share with the whole family. Luke included."

She doesn't look at all discouraged that she has to share and asks, "What is it?"

I hand her the bag and watch as she pulls out a baby doll wearing a T-shirt that reads, "My big sister loves me."

She holds the doll up to the family, and I smile at Ryder. "Go on," I say. "You tell them."

"We got Cora and Luke a baby brother or sister," he says with a chuckle. "We won't know which for a few more weeks, but sometime in October, you'll have a little sibling."

I'm not at all prepared for the uproar the announcement causes. I should have been ready to be swarmed by crying, laughing, smiling family, but every hug and every well-wish feels like a massive gift they're giving to me. Everyone at the party celebrates with us, but it's not until Cora starts demanding we sing happy birthday and have cake that my parents pull me into a corner of the kitchen.

"Baby," Ma says. She is sobbing, full-body sobs as she pulls me to her chest.

"I'm okay, Ma," I assure. "It's going to be okay."

"I know," she says, stroking my hair. "It's just… you're *my* baby."

My dad joins the hug, and by the time we're all cried out, Carol, Bev, and Sassy stampede into the kitchen to start talking about a baby shower, a gender reveal, where the nursery will be. Ma turns and looks at me.

"That's the other news," I tell my parents. And this is the hardest part of all. "I'm going to move in with Ryder and the kids. He wants to be there in case anything goes wrong, and I'd like some time for Cora and Luke to adjust to me before they have a new brother or sister."

My parents shock me by high-fiving. "One more out of the nest," Pops says.

"Dad," I blurt out, smacking him on the chest. "Seriously."

Ma laughs. "Honey, we've spent the last nine months trying not to hear you through the walls while you 'talk' on the phone. It's about time you two live under one roof. We might finally get some sleep again."

I'm blushing, and Ryder is nearly bent over laughing. Cora comes running in crying because she dropped her cake on the floor, and Ryder picks her up and carries her to the bathroom to wash her face.

"Let the sugar crash begin," he calls out as he leaves.

It's a perfect party.

A perfect day.

And a perfect life.

And this is just the beginning.

CHAPTER 21
GRACIE

SIX MONTHS *later*

Life changes fast. Quicker than I ever imagined.

A little over a year ago, I thought I'd never have a family of my own. I thought my body had robbed me of the opportunity. And when I met Ryder and fell in love with him and his two kids, I knew they were my family. I had everything I needed. I would think of the kids as my own, even if they didn't come from my womb. By all accounts, I'd be their mother for the rest of their lives.

But as with all things, life had other plans.

"He's so big," Ryder says, walking around the hospital room, rocking Ethan in his arms. "Way bigger than Cora or Luke."

"It's my Italian genes. We do everything bigger."

"He's going to be a rugby player," Ryder says, stealing a glance at me.

I shake my head. "I'm not sending my kid out there

on the battlefield. Rugby is vicious. He's going to be a drummer…something artsy."

Ryder laughs, not missing a beat with the rocking motion. "This is not an artsy kid. He's a footballer, babe. Through and through. Trust me."

I roll my eyes, too tired to argue with him about something that won't have a possibility of happening for years. "He's healthy. That's all I care about," I say on a yawn.

Ryder slides onto the bed next to me, and Ethan looks miniature in his giant arms. "He'll be whatever he wants to be."

"Now you're talking, buddy."

"He has your nose."

"Lucky him. He'll grow into it." I smile as I close my eyes, wanting nothing more than a nap.

There's a knock on the door before it swings open, and my parents walk in holding a bunch of balloons, wrapped presents, and a bouquet of flowers. "You awake?" Ma asks in a tone so loud that if I wasn't already, I sure as hell would be now.

"Yeah." I pull myself up in bed to sit up, trying to find the energy to be chatty.

"Come in," Ryder tells them when they don't fully walk into the room.

Ma looks at me for a second before her eyes dip to her newest grandchild. "Look, Mario. He's so little."

Pops smiles with a slow nod. "He's not that little, though, Lucia. He's a big boy. I see sports in his future."

Ryder turns his head toward me and smiles. "See."

"Yeah. Yeah," I mutter, waving the comment away with my hand. "We'll see. Maybe he'll be a tuba player."

My father winces. "Nope. Not him. He's like an Italian god. He's going to be a helluva tackle."

"I was thinking rugby," Ryder tells my dad as they set everything on the end of the bed except the flowers.

My father scrunches his nose. "No money in rugby."

"Sometimes things are bigger than money," Ryder tells my pop, and I know they're about to go ten rounds on if the love of a sport is more important than future earning potential.

Ma pulls out a vase from her purse like it's a normal thing to carry in there. "I brought these for you to brighten your room. It's so dreary in here."

"Thanks, Ma," I tell her, even though I don't plan to stick around long enough to let the gray walls have any effect on me. "You think of everything."

"How are the kids?" Ryder asks my mom as she fills the vase with water in the small bathroom inside my room.

"They're good. Excited. They barely slept last night. Vito is going to feed them breakfast and get them ready before bringing them over."

"Oh boy," I mumble. "That'll be interesting."

"He can do it. If not, it'll be a great learning experience. The way he plays around, he's lucky he doesn't have a half dozen little ones running around," Pops says as he moves to Ryder's side to get a better look at Ethan. "May I?"

Ryder doesn't hesitate in handing over our son.

My father takes him like a pro, supporting his head and holding him tight against his body. "My beautiful grandson," Pops says with so much pride. "I can't wait to watch you grow up."

Ma places the vase next to me on the small table they keep placing over my bed. "I'm going to spoil that baby rotten."

"Worse than Franco's kid?" I ask, thinking it's impossible.

Ma laughs as she moves the flowers around to make them look prettier. "You haven't seen anything yet."

"Our bank account is already in shock," Pops says, tipping the baby so my mother can see him.

My parents were there when he was born. They cried the moment their eyes landed on his face. I'd never seen them so happy. Not even when Franco's kid was born, but I'd never tell anyone that, especially my brother.

"I've made a decision," Ma announces as she takes the baby from my father's arms without asking. Surprisingly, he gives him over without even missing a beat. "I'm going to give up volunteering."

"Really?" I ask, completely shocked because my mother loves the time she spends in the community. I really think she enjoys the ability to hear the latest gossip from a variety of people.

Ma nods. "I'm going to start watching Franco's little one, and now that Ethan is born, I can watch him too.

Cora's welcome to join them at my house each day too, Ryder."

"Ma, no. You don't have to—"

"I know," she says, cutting me off. "But when you're my age, there's nothing more important than family. I want to surround myself with these babies for as long as I possibly can. Before you know it, they'll be going to kindergarten. I want to do it. Let me, Gracie."

"I'm not going back to work for a while, and when I do, it'll be part time."

"Then I'll take the baby part time, along with Cora."

"Are you sure you can handle three kids?" I ask and immediately regret the question.

Ma raises her eyebrow, the same way I do to everyone else when I want to challenge a bullshit statement. "You want to rephrase that?"

"I... Uh..." I shake my head and plaster on a fake smile.

Ma turns her attention to Ryder after a huff. "Are you okay with that, Ryder? Me watching the kids?"

Ryder shrugs. "Not a problem here. Cora will love that. She adores you."

"I adore that little girl too. It's nice to be able to spoil someone who can actually talk back to me."

And oh my God, do the two of them talk. My mom has finally found her soul mate for the gift of gab. The two of them can chatter for hours, bouncing from one topic to another, and none of it makes sense, but that doesn't stop them.

"It's set, then. When you head back to work, the kids will come to our house."

"Pops?" I ask because he hasn't said he's on board with it. "You want this?"

He grabs my hand and gives my fingers a squeeze. "It's been too quiet around the house since you moved out, Gracie. Between your mom and me, we can handle the kids, and it'll allow us to feel young again."

"I am young," Ma says to him.

"You'll always be young in my eyes," he tells her, schmoozing her like he always does.

"It'll give us a chance to spoil all the babies without you or Franco making a stink."

"I won't make a stink," I promise her. They spoiled me rotten, and I turned out okay. I expect them to do the same with their grandchildren. It would be weird if they didn't.

"I'm going to set up a little nursery."

My father rubs his forehead, muttering something I can't quite make out under his breath.

"The babies need somewhere to sleep when we watch them," she explains, somehow justifying the obscene amount of money she's about to spend. "You want them to sleep, don't you?"

Dad nods. "Of course, dear."

Ma looks to Ryder. "Does Cora nap?"

Ryder lets out a loud laugh, startling the baby. "I wish."

"Okay. Then we only need a crib."

"Only," Pops whispers.

Ma takes a finger and rubs the baby's cheek to calm him from Ryder's loudness. "Can I take the kids on field trips?"

"I guess," I say, but right now, I'd probably agree to just about anything.

"I promise I'll drive. It's safer that way."

My father grunts. "I drive just fine."

"When you can find your glasses," she teases him. "But I'm not risking the lives of my babies to those wonky orbs inside your head."

"My eyes are not wonky orbs."

Ma rolls her eyes. "Your prescription says otherwise."

Pops swipes his hand through the air before he collapses in the blue pleather chair across from my bed. "Whatever."

"So, I have a nursery to shop for and some field trips to plan." She smiles. "I'm going to show you everything. We're going to have so much fun. Just you wait, Ethan."

"Can I come sometimes?" I ask. "Or are adults not allowed to go on the field trips?"

Ma looks up with her eyes big. "You want to come?"

I raise a shoulder, feeling weirdly left out. "I mean, I like the museum and stuff too."

Ma smiles. "You're always welcome to come. You're my baby too."

And no matter how old I am, I know it's true. I'll always be their baby. Their little girl. After laying eyes on Ethan, I can't imagine the protective feeling that's buried in my gut ever going away.

"How about a family field trip once a month? There's plenty to do around here," Ryder adds because he clearly wants to go too.

"I like that," Ma says. "I'll ask Franco and Chloe if they want to come too. Vito and Benny, though..."

"They won't come. Don't bother," I tell her.

"I'll invite them. Maybe eventually they'll feel like they're missing out on something."

I pull the blanket up over my chest and wiggle my back against the world's most uncomfortable bed. "That'll never happen."

Ma walks around the bed and sits opposite Ryder with Ethan in her arms. "Your uncles are fuddy-duddies."

"Someday they'll settle down," Pops says, but there isn't a person in this room who believes that.

I busy myself with the extra-large water container they left with me, telling me I needed more hydration after labor. Which sounds great in theory, but that also makes me have to pee more than usual, and nothing about that is fun after pushing an abnormally large human out of that general area.

"Maybe your uncle will marry a different stripper this time," Ma says to Ethan. "One who wants to settle down and have a baby."

I choke on the water, and it dribbles down my chin as I quickly wipe it away. "Ma, that's awful."

She shrugs with a shitty smirk. "Well, where's the lie?"

"Lucia, you're rotten sometimes." Pops shakes his head and purses his lips.

"I'm always rotten, Mario. You know this, especially when it comes to my boys. They go where they let their penises take them, and it's never anywhere good."

"Ma, they may change."

"I'll be dead before that happens, Gracie."

"Two out of four isn't bad," Pops adds, trying to help, but Ma isn't having it.

She gives my father a wicked look. "I won't be able to rest until I know all my children are settled and happy."

"They're happy," Pops tells her.

"That they are," I say. "And they'll settle when they find the one person who makes them want to settle down. And if that never happens, if they never get married or have kids, I think Vito and Benny will still find ways to be happy. We all have different ideas of happiness, Ma."

She busies herself with Ethan, cooing over him as he sleeps in her arms. "At least I have you," she says to him. "I have four wonderful grandchildren to fill my life. What more could a woman want?" She stares down at Ethan like the sun rises and sets on his very presence.

Ryder scoots until his back is next to mine. He takes my hand in his as our arms are nestled between us. "Life's good," he says softly as my parents talk to each other about their two sons and their inability to find stable relationships.

"The best," I whisper, wondering if life will ever get better than this moment. I can't imagine it does.

This is the peak. The thing I dreamed about but wasn't sure would ever happen.

A child of my own and two more I love as if they were.

A family of my own.

And a man who loves me.

CHAPTER 22
RYDER

"CLOSE YOUR EYES."

Gracie stares up at me with her eyebrow cocked. "What's going on?"

I shake my head as I take her hands in mine. "It's a surprise."

"I hate surprises," she grumbles before finally complying. "If you scare me, I'm going…"

I squeeze her hands. "I'm not going to scare you, love. Let go a little bit and trust me."

She raises her chin, her face soft even if her eyes are sealed shut. "I do trust you."

"Good," I tell her, pulling her forward, careful to make sure she doesn't trip. "We're almost there."

"This is silly, Ryder. I've been to the falls a hundred times."

"Shush."

She jerks her head back but keeps her eyes closed. "Shush? I'll give you shush."

I've spent a month planning this day, working with her mother and our friends to pull this off. I even had her brothers in on it. The hardest part was keeping everyone quiet. There isn't much that happens around here without the entire town knowing every single detail.

We walk past the ice cream shop, standing at the top of the stairway down to the falls, where our closest friends and family are waiting. "Open your eyes, Gracie."

Her eyes flutter open, and a moment passes before she can get them to focus with the bright sun overhead. "What is this?" she asks as she takes a step forward to look over the railing. It takes her a second to spot her entire family waiting at the landing near the water's edge. "Ryder?"

I get down on one knee, doing something I wanted to do a year ago but didn't. Gracie made it clear that she wasn't ready to get married back then. But now we have a child together, we live together, and are married in every sense of the word except one.

Gracie turns slightly, her eyes searching for me before her gaze drops to where I'm kneeling. "Ryder?" she whispers.

"Gracie, I've never loved another person the way I love you. You've brought color back into my world, making every day full of light and life. I can't imagine spending a single day without you by my side. I love you, Gracie. Will you do me the honor of being my wife?"

Tears form in her eyes, and for the briefest of moments, I worry she'll turn me down. Weirder shit has happened to people. Maybe she still isn't ready and I am pushing the envelope with this elaborate plan.

EPILOGUE

RYDER

"I'M PROUD OF YOU, MAN," Austin says, adjusting my crooked tie.

I'm a mess. A bigger mess than I was when I married Elizabeth. I was too stupid and naïve back then to be nervous, but everything with Gracie is different.

"Why are you proud?" I ask, narrowing my eyes at my friend.

"You didn't give up. But then again, you never do."

"Quitting has never been an option."

"There he is," Lucia says as she walks over to me with her arms up, ready for a hug.

I welcome her embrace, knowing fighting it never works. Lucia gets her way no matter what, and it's easier and faster to give in.

"There's my new son," she whispers in my ear. "You've made me a very happy woman today. I wasn't sure my Gracie was ever going to get married."

I hug her tightly, knowing everything she does is out

of love, and she means every word of welcome into their family. Even before today, I felt like I belonged… almost like I'd always been there. "I'm honored she chose me."

Lucia pulls back and gazes up at me with the softest look. "She knew you were out there somewhere and wasn't willing to settle for anyone else, Ryder. You were worth the wait for all of us."

"You're too sweet, Lucia."

"Mom," she reminds me. "You're married now, which means you're my child too. Please call me Ma at least. Can you do me that small favor and make this old woman happy?" The way she's looking at me makes it impossible for me to say no.

She's been wonderful since the moment I met her. I don't know what I would do without the help she and Mario provide with the kids. They have always been able to fill in to watch them when I don't have anyone else to handle them.

"Yes, Ma."

My words instantly get me another squeeze. "You made me the happiest woman in the world."

"That would be me, Ma." Gracie glides my way, looking like an angel with sunlight behind her. When she gets to my side, she snakes her arm around my back. "I don't know what I did to deserve all this."

Lucia reaches out, placing her hand on Gracie's bare arm. "You deserve the world, sweetheart. Don't ever forget that."

Gracie tips forward and presses her lips to her mother's cheek. "I know, Mama. I love you."

"Love you too," Lucia whispers, smiling at the small, intimate gesture.

"Nonna, Nonna," Cora says, running toward Lucia at full speed, liable to knock her over. She's small but mighty, especially when she's using every bit of her energy and momentum.

But Lucia is prepared, having months of practice handling Cora. "Come here, baby," Lucia says, holding her arms out, leaning forward, and bracing for impact.

Gracie looks up at me with a smile, her eyes bright and filled with possibilities. "I can't wait for Ethan to be that age."

"Don't rush it. He'll be that age in the blink of an eye, followed by a mouthy teenager."

"He's not allowed to get that old."

I brush the backs of my fingers against her cheek. "We can't stop time, no matter how hard we try, but at least I'll have my best friend by my side for the journey."

"There's no one else I'd rather grow old with."

"I hope so. You're stuck with me now, Mrs. Cooper."

Her smile widens. "Today was perfect."

I peer up, looking over the small group of people we've invited to celebrate our wedding day with us as they laugh and enjoy the party. "I wouldn't change a thing."

This is my home.

It's where I belong.

Star Falls isn't just a small town; it's where I'm meant to be.

I have more friends and family than I ever thought possible. Finding peace is nearly impossible, but I'm never lonely anymore. I have an entire army of people to help me raise my kids, when I used to think I had to shoulder the stress alone.

And I have a wife, someone who loves me unconditionally, and I can't wait to see where the future takes us.

I hope you loved Never Too Soon and I can't thank you enough for reading. If you love the Bianchi family, there's more to come in **Never Too Close** - Vito's story.

Please ignore the stated release date of July 2024. It'll release sooner, but I don't have a firm date yet. I can't rush my creativity.

If you want to get the latest updates on my new book releases, join my newsletter at menofinked.com/news

Preorder Your Copy >> **TAP HERE...**
or visit *menofinked.com/ntc*

BE A GALLO GIRL...

Want to be the first to hear about the next Men of Inked book or everything Chelle Bliss? Join my newsletter by tapping here to sign up or visit *menofinked.com/inked-news*

Want a place to talk romance books, meet other bookworms, and all things Men of Inked? Join Chelle Bliss Books on Facebook to get sneak peeks, exclusive news, and special giveaways.

FREE EBOOK DOWNLOAD!

Looking for your next FAVORITE read?

Download **FLAME for FREE** and dive in. The family is waiting…

TAP HERE TO DOWNLOAD or visit *menofinked.com/flame* to grab your copy.

30 HOURS OF SIZZLING LISTENING!

visit *chelleblissromance.com* to get the complete Men of Inked Southside collection.

Olive Thornbury only had one crush in high school, and his name was Asher Gallo. She was smitten with him from the first time she had laid eyes on him. But instead of acting on how she felt, she kept her nose stuck in a book, finding safety in the words rather than emotions.

Asher had never thought of Olive as anything more than a friend. She was aloof, preferring to read books. instead of spending time with her friends. And when she moved away almost a decade ago, their friendship quickly disintegrated.

But when Olive returns to visit a local university, she never expected to run into a very grown up and even more handsome Asher. And what starts off as a rekindling of an old friendship turns into a fiery relationship.

Do the opposites have enough in common to go the distance? Or will their combustible chemistry cause the flames to turn everything into cinders?

Preorder your copy at *menofinked.com/cinder*

ABOUT THE AUTHOR

I'm a full-time writer, time-waster extraordinaire, social media addict, coffee fiend, and ex-history teacher. *To learn more about my books, please visit menofinked.com.*

Want to stay up-to-date on the newest
Men of Inked release and more?
Join my newsletter at *menofinked.com/news*

Join over 10,000 readers on Facebook in Chelle Bliss Books private reader group and talk books and all things reading. Come be part of the family!

Where to Follow Me:

facebook.com/authorchellebliss1
instagram.com/authorchellebliss
bookbub.com/authors/chelle-bliss
goodreads.com/chellebliss
tiktok.com/@chelleblissauthor
amazon.com/author/chellebliss
twitter.com/ChelleBliss1
pinterest.com/chellebliss10